Brutal

TITAN

E.V. OLSEN

Tropes and Trigger
WARNINGS

Tropes

RIVALS TO LOVERS, FORBIDDEN LOVE, BULLY MC, CLOSE PROXIMITY, DOUBLE BI-AWAKENING, PRIMAL PLAY, POSSESSIVE/PROTECTIVE MCS, TOUCH HIM AND DIE, SECRET RELATIONSHIP

Trigger Warnings

THIS BOOK CONTAINS SOME THEMES THAT MAY BE DISTRESSING TO READERS INCLUDING:

DESCRIPTIVE SEX SCENES, IMPACT PLAY, VIOLENCE/BULLYING, ROUGH SEXUAL PLAY, HOMOPHOBIC TERTIARY CHARACTER WHO MAKES HOMOPHOBIC REMARKS (APPEARS TOWARD THE END), MENTION OF SUICIDE ON THE PAGE, ONE MC PHYSICALLY ASSAULTED (NOT SA) ON THE PAGE (NOT BY LOVE INTEREST), DUBCON

Jackson

CHAPTER ONE

My fingers wrap around the waxed white laces of my skates, the rough texture biting into my skin as I yank them tight. It's going to be a tough practice, especially since we made it to Regionals.

And then there's the fact that those fucking Serpents made it too. The thought of facing off against them, against *him*, makes my blood boil. The memory of my knuckles connecting with Killian Blackwell's jaw, the satisfying crunch of bone against bone, and the sight of his blood splattering across his face, is still fresh in my mind.

I should've done more than just punch him. I should've wrapped my hands around his throat and squeezed until the life drained from his eyes. Maybe then he'd finally learn to keep his fucking mouth shut. However, I would've been suspended for the rest of the season . . . for the rest of my college career.

Maybe I should've signed the entry level contract with Winnipeg.

But I still wanted to be the big fish in the little pond, and they felt I could develop more. So, it was a mutual decision not to sign the contract after the draft. However, I doubt they'd follow through if I got arrested for murder.

Connor Walsh, our team captain, strolls over and plops down on the bench next to Alexei, my roommate and our top defenseman. "Eli still mad at you?"

Alexei shakes his head, his expression stoic as ever. "He got over it."

Viktor, our goalie and Alexei's cousin, lets out a bark of laughter. "He's mad at him for something else now."

I glance down at my wrist, flexing my fingers experimentally. The ache is still there, a dull throb that serves as a constant reminder of what happened last week. "And Alexei just fucks the tantrum right out of him."

My roommate pins me with a glare. "Maybe you should stop staying in the room when my boyfriend and I have sex."

I meet his gaze head-on, unflinching. "I live there too, fuckhead."

It's an old argument, one we've had a thousand times before. And it always ends the same way, with neither of us willing to back down. I'm not about to get kicked out of my own damn dorm room just so Alexei can get his rocks off with Eli.

Definitely won't mention it's kind of hot watching them fuck.

Not that I'm into guys. At least, I never thought I was. But there's something about their dynamic, something that intrigues me. Like the fact little Eli seems to have an invisible leash wrapped around my friend's neck.

And maybe I've perused a few gay porn sites. That did as much for me as threesomes have been lately, aka—not much. How's it possible to get bored of sex?

"Your hand getting any better?" Connor's voice cuts through my thoughts.

"Eh, still sore."

Viktor throws his hands up, his expression one of exaggerated frustration. "Can't believe I missed all the fun having to guard Feisty Mouse."

Our goalie is a bit unhinged. Not as much as our other friend, Zach Knight, who's one cold fuck. But Viktor is like a sociopath on crack some days.

While he might be complaining, we all know he enjoys spending time with his new best friend, latching onto him like an obsessive hellhound. They even have their own little group chat they call Bottoms Up.

"Blackwell got what he deserved," I say.

And he did. The Serpent's captain has been a thorn in my side for as long as I can remember, always there, always pushing, always trying to get under my skin. We've been at each other's throats since the day he showed up at hockey camp back when we were kids.

Seeing as he was from Massachusetts, I thought I'd never see him again. But over the years we'd play against each other at tournaments, and more often once we started playing at the junior level.

Now we're on rival college teams, only a handful of miles from one another.

We've always been on opposite sides of the ice.

Always fighting.

As if our endless feud is written in the stars or some shit.

Then, last week, the prick ran his mouth after the horn, bringing up the draft, reminding me of how far I fell. It was a low blow. One that I couldn't let slide.

I waited, took my time until after we got out of the locker room, then it was an all-out brawl. Fucking blood was everywhere.

The look on his face when my fist connected with his jaw, the shock and pain and anger, it was almost worth the ache in my wrist.

Almost.

A roll of clear tape hits me square in the forehead, jolting me out of my thoughts. Alexei snickers, his eyes glinting. "You fantasizing about slitting his throat again?"

I snort. "More like curb-stomping the piece of shit with my skate."

Walsh's nose scrunches. "Why would you wanna wreck your equipment on such a flea?"

Coach Nieminen's whistle blares through the locker room, the shrill sound cutting through the chatter and laughter. "You pricks ready for practice, or should I leave you behind?"

We all know it's an empty threat. Coach needs us, needs our skill and our talent and our drive. But that doesn't mean we're willing to push him. He has other ways of making our lives miserable, ways that don't involve benching us.

Plus, I kinda like him. I can see myself being a coach like him one day.

He turns to Alexei. "You get the information for your boyfriend?"

"Yeah, thanks."

Assistant Coach Buckland's lip curls up. Bastard always has a problem with us. Not sure why my father recommended him for the job. He's such a clown. But there's something about him, something that even unsettles Knight. And when the resident psychopath is bothered, there's a problem.

Not to mention his steely focus on me. For the past two years, the way he looks at me makes my skin crawl. But there's nothing I can do about it because outside of the stares, he's never done anything, never said anything not hockey-related to me.

I grab my helmet and stick, then head out of the locker room, the chill of the rink hitting me like a physical blow. I take a deep breath, letting the cold air fill my lungs, savoring the burn.

This is where I belong. On the ice, stick in hand, ready to do battle, ready to prove to everyone that I'm the best, that I deserve to be here, that I'm not just some late-round draft pick with something to prove.

I take a slow lap around the rink, letting my muscles warm up, letting the familiar rhythm of my skates against the ice soothe my nerves as I head over to the bench where Coach Buckland waits to run us through our first drill.

"Line it up!" he calls, his voice echoing through the empty arena.

I take my place at the front of the line, my heart pounding in my chest, my blood singing with anticipation. And when the whistle blows, I explode forward, my stick flashing as I corral the puck, my skates carving through the ice like claws.

"Not so fast," Walsh growls.

"Scared you can't keep up?"

While the five of us may be friends, it doesn't mean we won't fuck each other up. And we have at one point or another. It's how we know Knight's the most dangerous. He feels nothing.

Walsh is right on my tail, his breath hot on the back of my neck, his stick jabbing at my side. But I'm faster, stronger, better. With a twist of my wrist, I send the puck sailing into the net, the satisfying swish of the mesh music to my ears.

I turn, spreading my arms wide, soaking up the cheers and whoops from the rookies. They don't matter, but it riles Walsh up, so why not use it to my advantage.

He skates up beside me. "Cute trick."

The next round, I let Knight take the puck first, content to track him from behind. He's smooth, calculated, every move precise and deliberate. But he's too calculating, too predictable. And that's his weakness.

Right before the goal, I swing wide and clip the puck away, sending it through the targets quick as lightning.

Knight rounds on me, shoulders squared, his eyes cold and hard. "Blackwell still got your panties in a bunch?"

I roll my eyes. "You afraid of a little heat?"

"Were you even bringing any?"

Coach Nieminen's whistle rips through the air, sharp and shrill. "Cut the shit. Can't have anyone scratching due to injury at this point."

With a curt nod, I skate away.

Time to get my head back in the game and show Killian Blackwell, the Serpents, and the whole goddamn world what I'm made of, that I'm not just some late-round draft pick.

Even if it kills me.

Killian

CHAPTER TWO

I hold the door to Antonio's Subs open for our winger Raiyne, the blast of warm air from inside a welcome respite from the blustery winds whipping at our faces. He smirks, giving me an exaggerated curtsy before sauntering inside like he owns the place.

Sarcastic fuck.

The delicious aroma of toasted bread and melted cheese envelops me like a comforting hug as I follow him in. My stomach rumbles loudly, reminding me just how long it's been since I last ate. The cozy interior of the restaurant is packed with hungry customers, the red vinyl booths filled to capacity.

"I'm starving, Cap." Raiyne gives me a light punch on the shoulder. "You buying me dinner, right?"

I chuckle, shaking my head at his audacity. "Don't you ever buy your own shit?"

"With a pretty face like mine, never have to." He grins, dramatically batting his eyelashes.

"Pretty face, my ass."

Raiyne's far from ugly, with his sharp features and piercing hazel eyes. But there's something about him, a hint of danger that lurks just beneath the surface. It's like looking at a twisted version of Peter Pan, one you know instinctively to steer clear of.

Then again, most people seem drawn to that danger. They just don't realize that when it comes to Raiyne, there's no hint. He's all-out sinister.

Just like most of the Serpents.

Truthfully, I'm probably one of the tamer members of the team, sort of like their warden, keeping them in line and making sure they don't go too far off the rails. And I can't say they don't need it, especially when it comes to the monthly hunts in the Pine Barrens.

Raiyne studies the large menu hanging over the register, his brow furrowed. "Can't believe we're staying at the same hotel as the Titans."

Sometimes I wonder what I did to make the universe hate me so much. Why couldn't we be staying somewhere else? Sure, there are three other teams in our hotel as well . . . but the Titans.

That's just asking for one big murder scene. Hope the Providence police force is up to the task.

"Just remember why we're here." My voice is stern, which it needs to be to keep my teammates in line. Not that I'm any better, especially when it comes to Jackson Reed.

There's nothing I enjoy more than slamming that asshole into the boards, feeling the satisfying crunch of his body against the plexiglass. I've been doing it so often that I can still catch a whiff of his bergamot, oak, and sandalwood body wash when we're on the ice together.

Raiyne must be thinking the same thing because he pins me with a knowing stare, one eyebrow raised. "Like you don't want to find out which room is Reed's and break his leg?"

I can't help but chuckle. "No denying that."

"What did you say to him anyway? Seriously, he flips the switch if you just say 'Hi' half the time."

"Might have reminded him what a shit player he is. You know, seventh-round draft pick and all."

Not the smartest move, but I hated losing to them and just couldn't help myself. Especially after getting dumped the night before. Nothing like being told you're a boring lay to put you in a bad mood. But, as usual, the universe saw fit to have my now ex-girlfriend break up with me right before our game against the Titans.

Bringing up the draft was definitely a low blow, specifically since I'd gotten picked by the Rangers in the second round. Only my closest friends know the real reason I opted to go to college instead of signing the contract.

Reed ended up breaking my nose during the ensuing brawl. It wasn't the first time, and it definitely won't be the last fight we'll ever have.

The server at the counter greets us with a bubbly smile, her blond ponytail swaying. "What can I get for you guys tonight?"

"I'll take a large meatball sub, extra cheese and peppers," I say, my mouth watering. "And my friend here will have. . ."

"Make that two large meatball subs, extra cheese." Raiyne grins, rubbing his stomach.

Ten minutes later, walking across the parking lot, our food in hand and the warm scent of melted cheese wafting up from the bags, my footsteps falter at the sight of the five figures standing in front of us, dressed head to toe in black.

Jackson fucking Reed and his four friends.

If there's one group of people I hate more than anything, it's this one. Entitled rich assholes, with a healthy dose of psychosis to boot. They rival the Serpents in almost every way, except for one key difference—wealth. Not that anyone at our school is poor, but none of us are in the top point-five-percent of rich families the way these spawns of Satan are.

"What the fuck do you want?" Raiyne snarls, his voice dripping with venom.

"Just your friendly welcoming party." Jackson's gaze bounces from Raiyne to me, his light green eyes as intense as touching a bare wire. "Did you buy me dinner too?"

"Eat shit."

He just snorts, dismissing my weak comeback with a wave of his hand.

Jackson runs his hands through his wavy chestnut hair, and I turn my eyes from him to his teammate, who's bouncing on his toes like a deranged jackrabbit, a crystalline mask decorated like a demon nun—complete with an upside down cross—covering his face.

Viktor Novotny.

He, along with Connor Walsh and Zach Knight, are on a whole other level of dangerous compared to Jackson and Alexei Petrov.

I turn back to Jackson, my jaw clenched so tightly my teeth grind together. "Leave it for the games, asshole."

"Uh . . . no." He smirks, his eyes glinting with malice.

"So what? We're going to fight in the parking lot with cameras all around? Thought you were smarter than that."

Novotny chuckles behind his mask, the sinister sound sending a chill down my spine.

Jackson steps closer, invading my personal space. "Figured a celebratory hunt was in order. Thought you Serpents would appreciate the irony."

Fuck.

Raiyne's lips curl into an evil half-smile as his eyes glitter. Of course he'd like the idea. But I don't.

The Serpents hunt a different kind of prey, ones we've made sure deserve it. Because they don't walk out alive. I hardly participate—only when the victim has committed some atrocity that I'm truly passionate about punishing them for.

"Guess you two should start running." Petrov clenches and unclenches his fists, the veins in his forearms bulging. "Five, four—"

Jackson's smile turns wolfish, his gleaming white teeth bared. "Three, two-—"

God fucking dammit.

Raiyne drops his food, bending at the knees like he's about to take off sprinting.

"Reed, cut the shit. Now."

"Better run, bitch." His lips peel back into a snarl. "One."

I spin on my heels and take off running through the parking lot as fast as my legs will carry me, Raiyne to my left, matching me stride for stride.

"These fuckers are crazy." My teammate sounds both pissed and intrigued. "Can't believe they ruined dinner. I was really looking forward to that sandwich."

"Shut the fuck up and move your ass." I pump my arms harder, my heart slamming against my ribcage.

We dart between brick buildings and down alleyways hoping to lose the bastards, but their footsteps never cease pounding the concrete behind us. Up ahead is the dark outline of the woods, the same ones that run behind our hotel.

Without a second thought, I veer right, plunging into the tree line. But when I glance over my shoulder expecting to see Raiyne, he's nowhere to be found. The idiot must have gone left instead.

Fuck my life.

Last thing I need right now is for my friend to get hurt. However, when I slow down to double back, Jackson comes into view. So, I turn and head further into the woods.

Branches whip at my face and arms, the darkness pressing in around me like a living thing. My lungs burn with each gasping breath, and my legs ache. But I can't stop. I won't stop. Not until I'm sure I've lost him or until my body gives out.

Whichever comes first.

Jackson

CHAPTER THREE

When we found out the Serpents were staying at the same hotel, the temptation to fuck with Blackwell was too much. It was a bonus finding his teammate with him. Until freaky Peter Pan banked left and charged Connor, throwing his body at our captain's knees. Then he came out of the move like a goddamn panther and started running.

The other four took off after the piece of shit. But I stayed on Blackwell, chasing him into the woods.

Not the best move. A tree root can take us out just as easily being there's zero fucking light right now.

But it makes it more fun, and damn it, I'm hard as hell. No idea why. Maybe it's the chase. Or the promise of a good fight.

Who cares?

I'm amped the fuck up.

Ahead of me, Killian weaves between tree trunks. He's fast, a tad stronger than me if I'm being honest, but I'm more agile. It's the reason I evade most of his hits.

One on one, we're evenly matched. Same height, same build, probably same weight. It's why our fans love to watch us fight. The winner usually pulls some dick move or takes advantage of a miscalculation or slip in focus.

Like right now.

The golden blond-haired shithead looks over his shoulder, twisting a bit too much that he slows down a fraction, so I double my efforts and run full speed into him. He hits the tree trunk, and a roaring groan cuts through the night as he falls to the ground in a heap.

"Thought you could get away, dipshit?"

Before I can reach down and punch his golden boy face, something hits the back of my legs below my calves and I'm airborne until I hit the ground with a resounding thud.

"Fuck you, Reed." He launches himself at me and straddles my chest, knees pressed into my underarms.

Dammit.

Can't buck him off.

"What's the matter?" He looks like one pissed off tiger, especially with the blood trail running from the corner of his mouth to his clean, sharp jawline. "Look at you, trapped like a rabbit in a snare."

I move to dig my elbows into his inner thighs, but he grabs my wrists pinning them with one hand above my head. My dick throbs and twitches, my hips giving a little buck.

Killian slaps me. Hard. The sting and heat radiate outward. "Couldn't leave it for the ice. Couldn't let me have a nice fucking dinner with my friend. Why are you such a goddamn cunt?"

"You're the pussy who ran. At least your friend put up a fight." I twist and bite into his forearm, trying as hard as I can to break the skin beneath his shirt.

"Stupid fuck." He releases my hands but wraps his fingers around my throat, squeezing, his other arm cocked and ready to swing. "I'm going to rearrange your face so even God won't recognize you."

I glare up at him and smirk. "I'm an atheist. Fire away, motherfucker."

And he does. Once. Twice. And a third time.

"God, you're making my dick hard." It's not a lie. I'm harder than I've ever been. Even the orgy I took part in last month didn't get me this worked up.

He freezes, loosening his grip on my wrist.

Bad move, dumbass.

Only when I go to move, my eyes fall on the very defined outline of his erection. "Well, look at that. Color me intrigued."

Killian's honey-brown eyes follow my gaze down to his groin, then instantly he scrambles off me, tripping over his feet. "I'll color you in your own blood."

His threat has no real bite to it. Not for me, especially as he stands there, posture stiff, his broad chest expanding and contracting rapidly, breath fogging the air. I can't tell if it's from the chase or me pointing out he's hard.

But stumbling over his feet...The fucker's frazzled. My money's on the fact it's from the boner he's got going on.

My eyes drop again. "And here I thought *I* was the welcoming party."

"Shut up." Blackwell backs up, raking his hand through his mop of thick hair. "I'm not gay."

I laugh, loudly, throwing my head back and making it a spectacle. "You're not straight either. Your dick's practically trying to punch its way out of your pants. But hey . . . label yourself whatever you want."

"What's your excuse motherfucker? I'm not the only one sporting wood."

My dick twitches, most likely from the acknowledgement he's looking at it. So, I push my hips out a bit more, if only to fuck with him. "Like what you see?"

He snarls and steps back, creating more distance between us. "Go to hell, Reed. Find someone who actually likes cock and leave me the fuck alone."

He turns and runs off.

I spit blood on the muddy ground, wiping my face with the back of my wrist as I stare at that bubble ass of his. No sense in chasing him, not when I know where he's going.

Reaching down, I give my dick a squeeze to relieve some of the pressure. Never been so worked up in my life, and definitely not by a man.

But fuck, Killian Blackwell has me steeled and on the verge of coming in my pants.

Killian

CHAPTER FOUR

The scalding water cascades over my body, steam billowing around me, but it does nothing to calm the raging storm inside. My heart pounds against my ribcage, my blood thrumming with a desperate, aching need that consumes me. I close my eyes, my hand wrapping around my aching cock, and I lose myself in the sensation, stroking hard and fast, chasing the release that hovers just out of reach.

Images of Jackson flash through my mind—his intense green eyes, his angular jaw, the way his hard muscles flexed as we grappled in the woods, the way his wavy hair morphed from chestnut to mahogany when sweat-soaked. I should be disgusted, ashamed, but instead, I grow harder, my breath coming in ragged gasps as I fuck into my fist like a man possessed.

The pressure builds, coiling tighter and tighter until, finally, it shatters, and I'm coming harder than I ever have before, my knees buckling beneath me as I ride out the waves of pleasure. I slump against the cool tile wall, my chest heaving, my mind reeling.

What the fuck is wrong with me?

It's not the first time I've jerked off to him. Happened after our fight last week. Wasn't as intense, but still threw me for a loop.

Tried to pass it off as leftover adrenaline. Frustration, even. But it's . . . more than that.

Slowly, I straighten up, my legs still shaky beneath me. I turn off the water and step out of the shower, wrapping a towel around my waist. The bathroom is filled with steam, the air thick and heavy, and I struggle to catch my breath, my lungs burning with each inhale.

I stagger out into the room, collapsing onto the bed. The towel slips loose, but I don't bother to fix it, too drained to care. My mind is a whirlwind of confusion and self-loathing, and I bury my face in the pillow, trying to block out the world.

Thank God Trembley's out because I'm not sure I want to explain to my hotel roommate why I just went to town on myself.

My fingers curl around the wet strands of my hair and tug. Possibly being gay, or bi, or whatever is the least of my worries. It's how turned on I got when fighting with Jackson.

From being chased by him.

It's too fucked up.

And to make matters worse, the bite on my forearm is already bruising. The motherfucker marked me.

He's such an asshole. Always has been. An entitled prick who probably got a nose job to fix his perfect fucking features because I know I broke it when we fought at camp back when we were ten. There's also the time at the New England Sports Center when I made his nose gush blood during finals at the Haunted Shootout Tournament.

No way he's got some kind of miracle healing powers that it still looks perfect without surgical intervention.

Why does the fact he might have gotten a nose job bother me so much? Okay, that's probably the easiest to answer . . . because there's no evidence of all the times I kicked his ass over the years.

Someone knocks at my door and I get up to answer it, acutely aware of the towel still slung low around my waist, the damp fabric clinging to my skin.

Raiyne stands on the other side, his bottom lip split open and a mischievous glint in his eyes. "You made it back without a scratch. Figured you might be hungry."

I chuckle when he hands me a takeout bag from Antonio's. "Did *you* buy *me* dinner?"

"Should be the other way around since I had to take on four dickwads while only one went after you." He pushes past me into the room, flopping down on a chair near the window. "Petrov got me good."

I close the door and turn to face him. "How the hell did you get away?"

Raiyne throws his head back and lets out a full-bellied laugh, the sound echoing off the walls. "His fucking boyfriend!"

I tilt my head, blinking in shock as I wait for him to calm down enough to continue.

"The kid and his female friend literally pulled up in a car and got out yelling at Petrov. His boyfriend threatened to drive back to Long Island—wait for it—unless Alexei got 'in the car right fucking now'." Raiyne's face turns a dark shade of red as he laughs so hard he starts coughing, tears streaming down his cheeks. "Petrov actually gave in. Can you believe it?"

Petrov's boyfriend was at our last game against the Titans. He's tiny compared to the hulking Russian defenseman. I remember seeing the way they look at each other. My parents used to look at one another like that before my dad passed away and left my mom to fight her battle with muscular dystrophy alone. Well, not exactly alone since she has me and my sisters.

So, while my friend finds the whole situation hilarious, and I have to admit it's pretty funny, I can't help but see it a bit differently.

I put my sandwich down on the dresser, my appetite suddenly gone. "Lucky for you then. I'm surprised the others let you go so easily."

He shrugs. "Walsh didn't want to. He threw in some hits, but a few coaches from some of the other teams were around. Knight just appeared bored by the whole thing."

"What about Novotny?"

"Got in the car with Petrov, who seemed annoyed at that too." Raiyne juts his chin at me. "What happened with Reed?"

"Same old shit."

Lies.

But I don't want to get into it with him, don't want to admit to the confusing mix of emotions swirling inside me. While I'm close with a few of the guys on the team, I've never really opened up to them, never let them see beyond the carefully constructed walls I've built around myself.

Sure, they know about my mom, but only because she sometimes comes to games when we play in Boston in a wheelchair, while other times she doesn't. So, they had questions. But I never share how it affects me.

I don't want their sympathy, and I don't want my friends to look at me differently. Taking care of my mom and sisters is my duty, my privilege, and I wouldn't have it any other way. It's why I turned down the contract with the Rangers, why I chose to go to college instead. I need a degree to fall back on, something to ensure I can still provide for them even if my hockey career is cut short by injury.

"You okay?"

Fuck.

Guess I zoned out. "Was just thinking about how to get them back."

"Good, because I have a solution." He takes out an amber bottle labeled DHY Laboratories. "Shit's stronger than the average stink bomb. Not military grade, but it's up there."

Jesus, fuck.

"And what are we doing with that?"

"Stopped off at the hardware store and got some tubes. Figured we jimmy it under the door and pour this into their rooms. One of the rookies was able to get the Titans room numbers."

I run a hand through my hair, my mind racing. It's a damn good plan. Fucking with the Titans' sleep could cost them a win tomorrow.

Perfect.

After getting dressed in nothing but a pair of sweatpants—too hot for a shirt—Raiyne and I head down to the sixth floor where Jackson's room is. And he's rooming with Petrov. Don't know how one of our rookies got the information, and I don't really care.

Raiyne carefully gets a plastic tube under the door and luckily there's enough room that it doesn't squeeze closed.

I take the bottle and unscrew it, gagging immediately. "Jesus fucking Christ."

"Shh."

I pour the stuff into the funnel, holding my breath. Raiyne backs away holding his nose. Fucker. Leave me to do the hard shit.

"What is that smell? Oh, my god."

Raiyne snorts loudly, hand clamped over his mouth as he tries to keep from laughing. Part of me feels bad because that voice doesn't belong to either Petrov or Reed, which means it must be Alexei's boyfriend.

Oh, well. Date a Titan, expect to be collateral damage.

"What the fuck is that!"

Shit.

I drop the bottle and run just as the door is yanked open, while Raiyne's already turning the corner to the stairwell.

"Blackwell, you motherfucker!"

Behind me, Jackson's cursing as he chases me. Again.

My cock starts filling, and I slam into the door before racing up the stairs. Why is this shit getting me hard?

I make it to the landing and turn to go up the next flight just as the door crashes open, hitting the cement wall. Jackson and I lock eyes for a moment, jade against amber, and his lips curl up into a sneer. But my gaze also rakes over his shirtless chest, and my cock twitches.

Swallowing hard, I shake my head and continue running up to my floor, to safety because one thing's for sure . . . Jackson Reed is going to kill me if he catches me.

Arriving at the ninth floor, I race down the hall to my room, pulling my keycard from my pocket. But the fucking thing isn't registering. I tap it against the pad two more times until finally the little light turns green and the door unlocks.

However, Jackson slams into me with the force of a linebacker, both of us crashing to the ground inside the room, an empty fucking room.

"Looking to die, Blackwell?" Jackson mushes my face into the carpet. "Guess you didn't get enough earlier, huh?"

I arch my back, using the remnants of my energy to try to twist, then something heavy and unmovable lands on the middle of my back.

His knee.

The pressure is so strong, I think he'll break a few bones. While we may fight, and I don't mind rearranging his face, right now—I'm afraid.

Afraid he'll paralyze me.

Afraid by doing so, he'll take away my chance to play in the NHL.

Afraid he'll take away my ability to take care of my family.

Slowly, I turn my head to look over my shoulder. He's watching me, those eyes like green lasers, but he might as well be looking through me.

His face is feral, angry, unforgiving.

A brutal titan who probably doesn't know how to touch anything without the ruthless energy that emanates off him in menacing waves.

Jackson

CHAPTER FIVE

Can't say I'm not enjoying having Killian-bitch ass-Blackwell pinned under me, especially after he had the balls to stink up my damn hotel room. So much for being rested for tomorrow's game. At least we're playing a team we've wiped the floor with multiple times.

And chasing him got me hard and leaking again, igniting something primal in my blood. Fuck. What is it with my dick liking him so much? Seems it forgot to read the memo he's my enemy.

But that scared look he's got going on doesn't suit him. Killian's never backed down from me and this new development is sucking all the fun away. Time to kick it up a notch, get under his skin a bit.

I lean in close, until the ragged warmth of his breath hits my cheek. Slowly, deliberately, I drag my teeth over his earlobe, biting down just hard enough to pierce the skin. The coppery tang of blood hits my tongue and Killian makes a sound somewhere between a gasp and a growl, his hands flexing against the carpet.

"Miss me that much, asshole?" I murmur, my lips brushing the shell of his ear.

"Get the fuck off me." Killian's voice is strained, almost brittle, but I can feel the heat rolling off his body, the tension thrumming through his taut muscles.

"Nah. You look too good being pinned underneath me." My hand grips his nape, and I push forward, holding his face down to the ground. "Gotta say, that little stunt with the stink bomb? Pretty pathetic, even for you."

"Reed, I'm not gonna say it again. Get. Off." There's a waver in his voice, a hairline fracture in his trademark bravado, and it sends a dark thrill rushing down my spine.

I sit back on my heels, easing my weight off him minutely, and that's all it takes. Killian surges up like a wild thing, twisting and bucking beneath me until he manages to throw me off balance. We tumble sideways, grappling for dominance, a tangle of sweat-slicked limbs and heaving chests.

His fist slams into my cheek with a fury that's been building for the last few years. Somehow, he ends up on top, his knees bracketing my hips as he stares down at me with a mixture of rage and hunger, like a lit match to gasoline. "I hate you so fucking much."

"Feeling's mutual."

For a moment, we just stare at each other, bare chests heaving, the air between us electric with tension, but when I spot the delicious bruise on his forearm—my mark from where I bit him—I groan. He tilts his head, his golden blonde hair a wild tangle, and his pupils so large his eyes are almost black. His whole body is practically vibrating with barely contained energy, like a livewire.

I've never wanted anyone so much in my life. It's terrifying.

Slowly, deliberately, I angle my head up, my blood singing with anticipation. "Go on then, golden boy. Hit me again. See what happens."

He makes a sound like a wounded animal and then he leans down, his mouth crashing onto mine, hot and furious and devastating. His teeth catch my lower lip, biting hard enough to draw blood, and I groan into the kiss, my fingers raking down his back as he shifts until his body is flush against mine.

We tear at each other like brutal beasts, all tongues and teeth and desperation. Killian rocks his hips against mine and the friction is electric, like a lightning bolt of pleasure racing from my toes to my scalp.

I can feel him, hard and hot even through our pants, and my entire body throbs, my heart rate going through the roof. This is the first time I've had another dick against mine and . . . I fucking like it.

A lot.

I hook my leg around his and roll us over, pinning him beneath me once again, this time chest to chest. We're both panting, staring at each other with blown pupils and kiss-swollen mouths.

"Tell me to stop," I rasp and when he doesn't answer, I roll my hips, driving my erection into his. "Blackwell, tell me you don't want this."

But he doesn't say a word. Or can't.

Regardless, there' still some lines I won't cross.

Ever.

I grab his chin and squeeze. He hisses as I stare into his wide eyes. "Call it at any time and I stop. I'll beat you bloody, but I draw the line at non-consent."

He snorts, snapping out of whatever trance he'd been in a moment ago. "Murder good, rape bad."

"Exactly."

Killian swallows hard, his throat working. For a moment, I think he's going to push me away, but then he reaches up and fists his hand in my hair, yanking me down into another bruising kiss.

"Reed, just get your fucking hand in my pants before I change my mind."

Without wasting another second, I reach into his sweatpants and wrap my fingers around his hard length. Holy Mary, mother of fucks. Every cell in my body lights, my own dick leaking into my boxers at the feel of his hot skin in my palm. "You're . . . pierced?"

"Stop talking." Both of his hands grip my hips and his eyes flutter closed as his head falls back against the floor.

I give his dick a squeeze, his glorious abs twitching with his cock, then lean in until our mouths collide once more. Killian's tongue swirls around mine, warring, plunging, and sucking. He shouldn't taste so good, but I can't get enough.

"So hard for me," I say, nipping his jaw as my thumb grazes one of the barbells near his crown. "Fucking perfect."

"Didn't know you liked guys."

"First time. Now get my dick out." I lift a bit and the tiniest whimper leaves him, as if he hates the loss of contact, so I jerk him harder.

He wastes no time yanking my sweats down as far as he can get them, his calloused hand wrapping around me, moving from base to tip. My head drops down, resting on his shoulder as I buck into his fist.

God, it feels so fucking good I can barely breathe through it.

Killian chuckles. "Gonna blow already?"

"Fuck you."

"Not there yet."

We both freeze and I pick my head up, meeting his gaze. His mouth opens and closes for a second. "I . . . uh. Just being sarcastic."

I swallow hard, thankful he backpedaled because I'm not sure I want more than this. Maybe it's just an in the moment type thing.

Experimental.

Pushing my length against his, I wrap a hand around both of us and jerk. Roughly. A dash of pleasure thickens my dick, but it soars into an avalanche when Killian thrusts, rubbing me with his piercings.

By the third time, I'm thrusting as well, matching his rhythm and fucking my fist. Wetness slips beneath my fingers and I'm not sure if it's his precum or mine. Don't really care.

"Fuck, Reed." Killian is grunting, panting, moaning. But it's the way he says my name, all needy and gravelly that pushes me close to the edge. "Reed. Fuck. Reed . . . I'm coming. I'm coming. Jackson, I'm coming."

Watching his face as he orgasms, his fingers digging into my biceps as his cum coats my hand and our dicks, causes a fever-like sensation to spread throughout my body, my balls pulling tight, then I follow him over the edge embarrassingly fast. "Mother of fucks!"

My cum coats him, marks his skin, and a low growl erupts from deep in my chest as I thrust two more times, making sure to milk every last drop out of myself and onto the flushed golden boy beneath me.

Killian's hands drop from my arms as we stare at each other, breathing hard.

I push up and sit on my heels. "You look good covered in my cum."

His eyes narrow, gaze falling to my chest. "I marked you too, fucker."

I look down and sure enough, a few ropes of his cum are on my skin. The corner of my mouth ticks up slightly, then my brows furrow.

Since when do I like being marked?

Reality starts to seep back in, cold and sobering. I sit back against the wall, putting some much-needed distance between us. My body feels strange, wrung-out and oversensitive.

Killian also sits up and scoots back, rubbing his palms over his face. "This doesn't change anything. I still can't stand you."

"Right back at you."

A soft sigh falls from his lips as he shakes his head, cheeks flushing. "I've never even looked at another guy. Not even once. This . . . you . . . it's all new to me."

"I've watched some gay porn. Didn't do much for me. Not like watching my roommates." Okay, maybe I added the last part to cut the tension because a tandem freakout with my rival isn't happening.

"What the hell?" Killian stares at me, shock and disgust warring one another on his face.

I roll my eyes. "Not like that. Well . . . maybe like that. It's not my fault they go at it at two in the morning."

"Don't want to know any more about Petrov, thank you very much." He reaches for his waistband and pulls his sweatpants up, covering himself. "You need to go."

And I should.

Only, for the first time in three years, maybe ever, I feel completely satiated in a way that goes deeper than the physical. Like an itch I didn't even know I had has finally been scratched.

It's disorienting, and I don't have the first clue what to do about it.

"Jackson, get out." Killian's voice is quiet but firm.

Something in my chest squeezes at the dismissal. At the rejection. I stand and yank my pants up, then storm out of his room, knowing one thing with a cold certainty—this isn't over.

Not by a long shot.

Killian

CHAPTER SIX

The Dunkin' Donuts Center vibrates with anticipation as the Titans glide across the ice in their pristine white away jerseys, their skates carving elegant paths through the fresh surface.

Raiyne, some of the guys from our team, and I grabbed an early breakfast before heading over to scope out the competition.

It's a common tactic, watching other teams play, looking for weaknesses to exploit or strengths to counter. And yet, my focus isn't on Crestwood University's hockey team. It's entirely on one player, his name a drumbeat in my head, a fever I can't shake.

Jackson Reed.

My eyes track his every move. He's poetry in motion, all coiled power and deadly precision, and I can't look away. My heart beats out of control, as if someone injected me with a liter of adrenaline.

When his head snaps my way, his light green eyes locking onto me like a targeting system, my breath catches in my throat. For a moment, the world narrows down to just the two of us. But then his lips twist into a scowl and he pivots sharply, skating to the far end of the rink like he can't get away from me fast enough.

"Damn, that's new." Trembley claps my shoulder. "Since when does Reed avoid us?"

Since we rutted against each other like animals in heat, our hands desperate and greedy, our mouths hot and filthy. Since I came harder than I ever have in my life, my vision whiting out with the force of it.

Since I kicked him out of my room with his cum still cooling on my skin.

It was a dick move, but my head was spinning, and I had no idea when Trembley was coming back. Last thing I needed was to try to explain having a sexual encounter with our biggest rival while I'm still trying to figure it out myself, including the fact that I apparently like men.

And that I specifically really like Jackson.

Maybe I *only* like him.

I swallow hard, my throat dry. "Who knows what goes on in that guy's head?"

It's a weak deflection, but Trembley just shrugs, his attention drifting back to the ice as the game gets underway. I try to focus on the play, on the clash of bodies and the spray of ice, but my mind keeps circling back to last night, to the heat of Jackson's skin against mine, the ragged sound of his breath in my ear.

My thumb lightly grazes over the bruise on my forearm as I shift in my seat, my jeans suddenly feeling too tight. I can still feel the ghost of his hands on me, the bruising grip of his fingers, the hot slide of his tongue. It's like he's branded me, left some indelible mark I can't scrub away no matter how hard I try.

And believe me, I've tried.

I spent an hour in the shower after he left, the water scalding hot, my hand working between my legs, chasing the high of his touch. But even as I shuddered through my release, biting down on my fist to muffle my cries, it wasn't enough. It was like an itch I couldn't scratch, a hunger that gnawed at my bones.

I'm jolted out of my spiraling thoughts by a roar from the crowd. The Titans' goalie goes into a front split, blocking the puck, then catches the rebound.

"Novotny is on fire. We need to figure out a weakness. Seems he's been working on not committing too hard to the right side anymore," Raiyne says.

We could always capitalize on the Titans' goalie committing to the right side, but so far he's balanced, making him harder to beat.

Viktor Novotny is awesome. Even got drafted to the Islanders during the second round. Not sure why he hasn't signed yet. Unless it has to do with his behavior. The motherfucker is as unhinged as they come.

And proud of it.

My eyes snap back to Jackson as he cuts through Cornell's defense like a hot knife through butter, his skates flashing as he dekes left, then right, leaving his opponents grasping at air. He passes the puck to Walsh with a flick of his wrist and Walsh one-times it toward the net.

The Cornell goalie makes the initial save, but he can't control the rebound. The puck bounces off his pads and straight onto Jackson's waiting stick. Jackson doesn't hesitate. With a quick snap of his wrists, he buries the puck in the back of the net, the red goal light flashing as the crowd erupts in cheers.

I want to cheer too, want to celebrate the sheer artistry of the play, but I can't. So, I settle for watching the fierce joy on Jackson's face as he rounds the net, his teammates crashing into him in celebration. He's magnetic, incandescent, and it makes something clench deep in my chest, something that feels an awful lot like longing.

God, I'm so fucked.

The game wears on, the two teams trading blows like heavyweight boxers. The Titans are dominating, their skill and cohesion evident in every play, but Cornell refuses to go down without a fight. The hitting is fierce, bordering on dirty, and the ref's whistle seems to be glued to his lips as he calls penalty after penalty.

"One of the d-men should take Reed out. Little trip close to the boards, make him think twice about dangling like that."

Not sure which of my teammates said it, but my fingers dig into my thighs hard enough to bruise, and it takes everything I have to not spin around and deck someone.

It's irrational, this sudden surge of protectiveness. Jackson is more than capable of taking care of himself. But that doesn't stop the snarl that builds in my throat, the harsh "Fuck off" that spills from my lips before I can bite it back.

Raiyne blinks at me, his brows furrowing. "You okay?"

"Yeah, just didn't sleep well."

It's not a lie, exactly. I slept for shit, tossing and turning until the sheets were tangled around my legs because every time I closed my eyes, I saw Jackson's face, felt the weight of his body on mine.

Raiyne's expression softens. "Heard you talking to your mom when I passed by. Wanted to make sure you got away after the prank. Didn't want to eavesdrop, so I left, but is everything okay with her?"

I swallow past the lump in my throat, my chest tightening with a complicated mixture of love and guilt and gratitude. Raiyne's a good friend, the best, and I hate lying to him. But I'm not ready to talk about this thing with Jackson.

"Yeah, she's doing all right," I manage, my voice rough. "Having a few good days, which makes it easier to be up here, you know?"

It's the truth, mostly. Mom's health is as stable as it ever is, her good days outnumbering her bad ones for a change. But I called her because I needed to hear her voice, needed her steady reassurance and unconditional love. I needed to know that even if everything else in my life is shifting beneath my feet, she'll still be there to catch me if I fall.

And she was.

She listened patiently, all too happy to hear about what was going on with Jackson—more so than I'm comfortable with. The woman even teased and asked when I was bringing him by to meet her, referring to Jackson as my *boyfriend*.

Like that would ever happen.

But she held no judgment, just listened, assured me she'd support whatever I decided was right.

On the ice, the Titans are up by three goals by the end of the second period. Jackson made some errors, including a blind pass that ended up with Cornell scoring.

"Are they even trying? Looks like they're playing as if it's just a practice." Trembley stretches, then pulls the bill of his cap down as if he's about to take a nap. "Expected more from them. This shit's kinda tame."

"Next period will be brutal. Things always go sideways when one team is getting their ass whooped."

Raiyne's not wrong. And, true to his prediction, the third period is chippy as hell. Unfortunately for Cornell, that means the Titans' leashes came off. Both teams have two men in the penalty box consistently. Minor and major penalties are being handed out like candy on Halloween.

And with the amount of blood being spilled on both sides, you'd think this was a blood drive instead of a hockey game.

Petrov sends the puck into the offensive zone and Jackson chases it down in the corner. Then Cornell's biggest defender charges and cross-checks him into the boards, the hit vicious and dirty. Jackson crumples to the ice, his body going limp, and for a moment I swear my heart stops beating entirely.

I jump to my feet, a bit too fast to come across as curious. Bile creeps its way up my throat when Jackson doesn't get up right away. Fuck, he may be knocked out.

Then the defender brings his stick down on Jackson's side in a brutal slash.

A menacing sound, almost like a roar, bellows up from deep within my chest as I punch the plexiglass. "Motherfucker, I will end you!"

I don't even see Jackson anymore, my focus solely on the dead fuck who's grinning. "You're dead, you hear me? You're fucking *dead*!"

I slam my fist against the plexiglass again, and again, and again, the pain barely registering through the haze of my fury. I want to rip that smug motherfucker apart with my bare hands, want to make him bleed and beg and *hurt* for daring to touch what's mine.

Raiyne lays a hand on my shoulder. "Killian?"

"Jesus, Blackwell. You okay?" Trembley juts his chin toward the glass, and fuck, there's blood on it.

I look down at my hand and sure enough, I split my knuckles open. My teammates look at me, a mixture of concern and curiosity on their faces. But not the good kind. More like the 'you have some explaining to do' kinda way.

My body shakes and I turn back to the ice. Jackson's staring at me, his eyes full of confusion, shock, and something else, something raw and vulnerable that makes my breath catch in my throat.

But then he blinks and it's gone, his expression shuttering closed as he pushes himself to his feet, shrugging off his teammates' concerned hands.

"I need to get out of here." I shove past my teammates and exit the arena before I do something stupid because seeing Jackson hurt, seeing him vulnerable, unleashed something dark and possessive and terrifying inside me.

Something that roars *mine, mine, mine* and makes me want to rip the world apart to keep him safe.

I snort and shove my hands into the pockets of my sweatshirt.

Just because some of my cum marked him doesn't make him mine.

Only, the primal part deep inside calls bullshit. The same part that wants revenge against Cornell because no one gets to hurt Jackson but me.

Killian

I collapse onto the bench in the locker room after showering, my chest heaving and my muscles trembling with exhaustion. The game against Penn State was brutal. Took everything we all had to squeeze out a win.

"Want to tell us what's gotten into you?" Trembley stares at me while putting on his sneakers. "You were like the goddamn Punisher out there."

"It's Regionals. Not holding back."

My response garners eye rolls from him and Raiyne. I glare at the both of them, taking a deep, measured breath. "Got something to say?"

Leave it to Raiyne to stir the pot. "Seems like you're pissed because someone almost broke your play toy this morning."

My jaw clenches, a muscle near my eye twitching. I take a second to figure out how to play this, then keep my tone deliberately casual. "What can I say? Going against Reed always pushes me to be better—like a natural performance enhancer. Can't have him benched when we face off against the Titans."

Yeah, they're not buying my bullshit.

Trembley stands, crossing his arms in front of his chest. "That the reason you damn near broke your hand? 'Cause call me stupid, but then *you'd* be benched, right?"

I put my sweatshirt on then flick him off. "Between hockey and my family I've got enough on my plate. Don't need you two jackasses adding to it."

Raiyne opens his mouth to say something but backs off. As mischievous and menacing as my friend can be, I pulled the low-blow card, aka the mom card. His face pinches together and he lets out a huff.

"We're going for pizza. You coming?"

I shake my head. "Nah, gonna head back to the hotel. Ice my hand a bit." I know they mean well, but the last thing I want is to be around anyone, so I give a small nod and smile, then turn and head out.

Back at the hotel, I spot Petrov and his boyfriend leaving as I arrive. I *should* go and ice my hand, but this might be the only opportunity to check on Jackson, and I need to see him. Need to make sure he's okay. I just hope he's back in his old room, otherwise I have no idea where to look.

The elevator ride to Jackson's floor feels like an eternity, my heart hammering against my ribs with every passing second. When I finally reach his door, I hesitate and stand in front of it for ten minutes, listening for any movement inside before I finally knock. A week ago, I'd be banging on it, cursing him out. But now, I'm shuffling from foot-to-foot, talking myself up.

The door swings open and Jackson stands there, his posture relaxed but his eyes sharp and assessing. He's wearing a pair of gray joggers that cling to his muscular thighs and a maroon T-shirt that stretches across his broad chest. The sight of him makes my mouth go dry, my pulse picking up speed.

"To what do I owe this visit?"

I swallow hard, trying to find my voice. "Can I come in?"

His eyes narrow, his head tilting to the side. "Why?"

"Wanted to see how you're doing after that hit this morning." I shove my hands into my pockets, feeling awkward and exposed under his gaze.

"Why?" He leans against the doorframe, blocking me.

"Reed, stop being an asshole. I'm . . ."

This is a bad idea. But when I turn to walk away, he grabs my upper arm. The sleeve of his T-shirt shifts and I spot the bruises on his bicep, ones I left there from squeezing so hard the night before, and I damn near groan.

"Gonna come in your pants?"

My gaze shoots up and meets his, but he laughs and walks away, pushing the door open. An invitation. One I take.

"Guess you marked me with more than just your cum. Sneaky bastard."

I rub the back of my neck, unsure of how to respond, especially because my cock is starting to swell. Sex isn't why I came here, but goddamn if it's not on my mind now.

He half sits on the dresser, eyeing me. "You good?"

I blink a few times, forgetting how to speak.

Jackson just laughs. "Since when do you get all flustered?"

Clearing my throat, I stand taller. "Just came here to make sure you're okay. Don't want to accidentally kill you on the ice." He snorts, so I wave a dismissive hand in the air. "I said accidentally. Purposely killing you is still on the table."

Jackson pushes off the dresser with a slight wince. "Said I'm fine, Killian. You didn't need to come check up on me."

"I know." I rake a hand through my hair, frustration welling up in my throat. "I just . . . I needed to see for myself."

Something flickers in his eyes, there and gone too fast to decipher, but then his gaze drops to my hand. He steps closer, his fingers brushing over the damaged skin and the touch sends a shiver down my spine. "You really did a number on the glass this morning."

"I couldn't just stand there and watch him hurt you." The words slip out before I can stop them, too honest, too raw.

"You can't say shit like that," he murmurs, his voice low and rough. "Not when I'm trying to hate you."

I let out a shaky laugh, my hands coming up to grip his hips. "Think we're a little past hate at this point."

He groans. "Didn't care to see your pretty face looking so distraught."

"So, you think I'm pretty? Is that what gets you all hard?"

Jesus, fuck. Where'd that come from?

As if someone else just invaded my body, I follow up with, "Or do you like the way my pierced cock feels. Bet you'd scream like a whore with it up your ass."

Jackson erases whatever distance is between us, grabbing my hair. "Listen, you jerk off. If anyone's screaming, it'll be you when I fuck you so hard you forget your damn name."

The scent of bergamot, rich oak, and sandalwood fills my nose and I inhale deeper. My cock is steeled, pulse thrumming in my ears. I lean in and bite his bottom lip, reaching down and palming his groin. "This all for me?"

"Think you can take all of it?" Between his tone and that sly smirk, he's mocking me.

"I'm bigger, and we both know it."

He yanks my head back by my hair, his teeth sinking into my neck. My hips buck against his thigh and I start grinding. He grunts low and pulls back, a wolfish smile spreading across his face. "Fuck, Blackwell, so goddamn needy."

And as if proving him right I grab his wrist, pulling it out of my hair, then slam my mouth down on his and moan against his lips.

He moves forward, backing me up to the bed, unbuttoning my jeans as we go. "This is such a bad idea."

"The worst," I agree just as Jackson grabs the hem of my shirt and pulls it up and off. "We should stop."

"We should," he echoes, but his hands are everywhere, sliding over my chest, my arms, my back. His touch is electric, igniting sparks under my skin until I'm burning with it, aching for more.

He pushes me down onto the mattress, then I help him take my jeans off because fuck, while I'm not sure what I'm doing, right now, all I want to do is bury myself inside him and see the sounds my Jacob's ladder can rip from those pillowy lips.

Once my boxers are off and I'm on full display, his gaze rakes over me before he sheds his clothes. I catch the momentary fault when he removes his shirt, the way he winces.

He's injured.

It can't be that bad, though. Otherwise, he'd be kicking me out.

I sit up, scooting my knees under me, my cock pointing straight up. But instead of joining, he walks toward a bag in the corner and rifles through it, returning a moment later with a bottle of lube and condoms.

"Why do you have that?"

"Who said it's mine?" He tosses the items onto the bed, then lunges forward, attacking my mouth.

"Ugh, we're using Petrov's—"

His palm smacks my ass so hard I jerk forward, pressing myself into him. "Say another man's name again and see what happens."

I look right at him and in the sluttiest voice—or at least what I think a slutty voice would sound like—say, "Petrov."

Jackson's entire face turns furious, but when he moves, I twist to the side, then pull his knee out so he lands onto the mattress on his stomach. Quickly, I mount him, laying my full weight on him, my chest to his back.

I chuckle, nipping his ear. "Like I said, I'm going to be the one fucking you."

A growl tears from his throat. A literal growl. Like a goddamn wolf. I expect him to fight me, to try and flip me. Instead, he pushes his ass up into my cock and moans.

"Like that, baby."

Who the fuck am I right now? And why did I just call Jackson Reed baby?

He hides his face in a pillow and pushes against me again. This time I grind down, my cock sliding between his muscular cheeks. "Fuck, Reed. Are we really going to do this?"

Jackson turns his head, glaring at me over his shoulder. "You stop now and I *will* smash your skull into the wall until your brains spill all over the carpet."

I bite his shoulder, chuckling. "You say the most romantic things."

"Shut up, asshole."

My hips cant against Jackson, precum making his crack slippery. My breaths grow shallow, fingers digging into his hips. He writhes beneath me, most likely fucking into the bed. "Your cock aching, baby?"

His nails raking into the skin of my thighs as he scratches up, releasing the filthiest moan I've ever heard.

"Is that a yes?"

Instead of answering, the asshole turns and bites my forearm, hard, marking me yet again. I return the favor on his other shoulder.

Guess we've traded bruising one another with punches for doing it by biting.

When I sit up, the tiniest whimper escapes his lips and he buries his face into the pillow again. I swat his ass. "I heard that."

He holds up a hand and gives me the finger. Shaking my head, I reach over and grab the lube and condom. Clicking the top open, I slick my fingers up.

After our encounter the other day, I found myself on the internet hoping to find something about what I'm going through in regards to my sexuality, kinda even wished there was some sort of miracle answer out there.

Curiosity also got the better of me and I started reading about having sex with a man. It was a bit overwhelming, especially when it came to preparing for it. There were different opinions about so many things.

But I still found myself wanting to try . . . with Jackson.

Jackson looks over his shoulder at me, a deep flush covering his neck and cheeks, his pupils blown. His lips are pursed, a slightly angry look on his face. "Are you going to fuck me or just sit there like you're deciding what to order from the menu?"

I laugh so fucking hard I temporarily forget what we're about to do, then I look at him and quirk a brow. "Well, there are options."

"Blackwell!"

"Impatient much?" I spread him and my cock leaks an absurd amount of precum when my eyes fall on his clenching and unclenching hole.

My fingers slip between his cheeks, one pushing its way inside his body. When I meet resistance, I look up. Jackson's eyes are closed, mouth agape, fingers white knuckling the sheets.

"Want me to stop?"

"No."

After a few breaths, he relaxes and I push inside. He's smooth and warm. Different than a woman yet familiar. "Fuck, you're tight."

"Add another finger. Now. Work me open."

"I . . . how?"

He shakes his head, face buried in the pillow once again as he scoots his knees under him, opening up for me. "Don't know. Just do something. Now."

Pushing two fingers into him, I curl them and he pushes back, moaning loud. My cock is painfully hard, aching to be inside him. When he starts fucking my fingers, I withdraw them, tear open the condom and roll it on, then slick it with lube.

His fingers tighten around the pillow as he arches, lifting his ass higher.

Seeing him like this snaps what little restraint I have. Grunting, I thrust inside Jackson hard enough to rip a strangled cry from him. It's barbaric, selfish even. His body is tense and shaking, a sheen of sweat coating his skin.

"Fuck, sorry."

He doesn't say anything, just grips the pillow tighter. After a minute or two, he starts to squirm. I carefully pull out, then push back in, setting a steady pace.

My eyes close as I relish the feel of him, the way he squeezes my cock. Nothing's felt this good before, especially when he starts throwing his ass back into me.

"More . . . harder. Faster. Fuck me." Jackson continues to beg through gritted teeth, and while I try to comply, it's not enough. He plants both hands on the mattress and uses it as leverage as he drives his ass back even more. "Killian! Fuck me, dammit! Fuck me so hard I can't talk!"

With a snarl, I reach around and grab his throat, pulling his back to my chest as I fuck into him. "Feel good, baby? This how you want it?"

"Harder!"

I bite, suck, and choke him as I give him what he wants until I'm railing into him like a feral beast strung out on crack. Reaching around, I grab his weeping cock and jerk him hard. "Fuck my fist. Get yourself off for me."

And he does, driving into my fist, then backward onto my cock. His hands clutch my forearm as I squeeze his throat, his moans and the sound of my hips slamming into his ass, filling the room.

"I'm . . . Kill . . . Oh, shit . . . Kill, Kill . . . coming!"

Jackson shouts and clenches around my cock, punching my own orgasm from my body. My hand leaves his throat and wraps around his chest, pulling him against mine as I hold on for my life while pure bliss floods my system. Jackson locks up, a cry instantly dying on his lips.

I fuck into him, using him like a toy, grunting and shouting until I start emptying into the condom.

When my orgasm subsides, I soften my grip and pull free. "God, I've never fucked like that before."

Jackson doesn't say anything and his body's still tense and shaking, sweat dripping down his spine.

"Hey, you okay?" This doesn't feel right. "Jackson?"

"I'm fine. Just . . . clean up and go. Alexei and Eli should be coming back."

When I grip his shoulder to turn him around, he pulls away. A lump starts to form in my throat, and when he continues to avoid looking at me I get up and go to the bathroom, taking care of the condom and cleaning up.

Jackson meets me at the door, shoving my clothes at me. His nostrils flare, eyes narrowed. But I catch the way his bottom lip trembles. "Jackson—"

"We fucked. Now leave."

"You're such an asshole." I snatch my clothes from him and get dressed. His chest heaves as if he's barely containing his anger so I don't even bother putting my shoes on. Pulling the door open, I sigh and turn back. "Are you okay? Did I—"

The bastard shoves me into the hall and I fall on my ass, the door closing. To make matters worse, Petrov and his boyfriend are a few feet away staring at me.

Fuck if I don't want go back inside and beat the ever-loving shit out of Jackson, but the way his lip trembled, I can't help but think I did something.

Hurt him somehow.

My throat tightens, and I lift myself up off the ground, then make my way to the elevator. Last thing I need is to lose my shit in front of Petrov, especially after he just watched me get tossed on my ass.

I smash the button for my floor, then punch the wall. Of all the people in the world, why did I have to want Jackson Reed?

Jackson

CHAPTER EIGHT

The second the door clicks shut, I rush into the bathroom and vomit. But that only makes the pain worse. Each heave sends bolts of agony lancing through my torso, stealing my breath and blurring my vision.

I clutch the porcelain, my knuckles white and my forehead pressed against the cool plastic, trying to will the pain away through sheer force of stubborn determination.

But it's no use. The throbbing ache in my ribs is a constant, pulsing reminder of the hit I took this morning, the one I've been trying so hard to ignore. My ribs crackle with each shuddering inhale, a sickening counterpoint to the pounding of my heart.

I can't hold back the tears that slide down my cheeks, hot and shameful. I'm Jackson fucking Reed. I don't cry. But here I am, sobbing like a child because it hurts, it hurts so fucking much and I don't know how to make it stop.

My ribs have got to be broken. Can't deny it anymore. There's no way this amount of pain is just from them being bruised. But we still have games to play and like fuck am I going to sit on the bench.

Didn't count on Killian coming by either. Definitely didn't count on how good it would feel to have him inside me, stretching me, claiming me, only to have that euphoria shattered by a blinding burst of agony when his arm tightened around my chest.

Every inch of my body throbs in time with my racing pulse. And beneath that, a new ache is making itself known. A deep, insistent throbbing from where Killian pounded into me.

Jesus Christ, my ass hurts.

Okay, that one's my fault. And Killian's. The motherfucker railed into me like a beast, and I loved every minute of it until his stupid arm squeezed the ever-loving shit out my ribs.

Ruined my damn orgasm. All the pleasure I felt vanished into blinding pain. Think I may have passed out for a second, which is why the moment he finished, I kicked his ass out.

What eats at me more than this pain . . . the hurt look on his face. Same one I probably had the night he kicked me out.

The hotel door clicks and I try to get up, but I'm too slow. Alexei and Eli come rushing over a second later and help me to the bed, their touches careful, almost reverent. Like I'm something fragile, something breakable. It makes me want to scream, to lash out, to prove that I'm still the same old Jackson, indestructible and untouchable.

Alexei stands to his full height. "I take it your dumbass lied to the trainer."

It's not a question. He knows me too well, knows my stubborn pride and reckless disregard for my own well-being.

I try to shrug, but even that small movement sends daggers of pain radiating out from my ribs. "Don't want some stupid doctor benching me for the rest of the season."

Alexei shakes his head. "Buckland was muttering some nonsense. Swear the fuckhead even smirked seeing you go down."

My jaw clenches. Not sure what's up our assistant coach's ass, but he'd made a comment to me about playing like garbage. Granted, none of us were really giving it our all against Cornell. Didn't really need to. We were reserving our energy.

And after the hit, when I needed a little extra help getting on the bench, the asshole was rougher than he needed to be, as if he wanted to cause me more pain.

Eli hovers at the foot of the bed, his big eyes filled with worry like some freaked out momma bird.

"Stop staring at me like that. I'll be fine." I fold the blankets over my lap. No doubt I look like shit, but I'm also naked.

"How bad is it?"

I scrub a hand over my face, wincing—even that small movement jostles my battered torso. "Pretty sure they're broken. But if I tell Coach, I'm out. So keep your mouth shut, yeah? I can handle it. Just need something to take the edge off."

Eli searches my face, gnawing on his bottom lip, a sure sign he's got something to say.

"Spit it out. You're thinking so loud I can practically hear the gears turning."

Alexei growls and grabs him by the hair, yanking his head back. "Keep your mouth shut."

I look between them and hate that they seem to be speaking to each other without actually talking. "Keep his mouth shut about what?"

Alexei must tighten his grip because Eli whimpers, though I'm not sure if it's from pain or being turned on. Feisty Mouse—fuck Viktor because now we all call him that—likes when my friend is rough with him.

"Nothing," Alexei says as he wraps his arms around his boyfriend.

"Bullshit." I look back at Eli, who's staring at the floor. "I take back liking you enough to not want to kill you."

Of course Alexei snarls, glaring murderously at me.

"I'll kill you too. Bury both of you in the same grave if you want. Now spill it."

"We've been back for at least twenty minutes," Eli blurts out.

"Okay?"

"Shut it, Solnyshko."

But Eli just ignores him. "We heard you having sex, then saw you push Killian out of the room. You know he fell, right?"

Oh.

Fuck.

Alexei's jaw clenches, and his nostrils flare. "You thought getting railed was a good idea in your condition? Knew you were reckless but didn't realize you were actively suicidal."

"Who said—"

"The way you sat down and shifted, more than just your ribs hurt." Alexei waggles his stupid brows and I want to punch his stupid face, but he continues. "Figured you'd be the one fucking him."

Me too.

Eli pulls away from his boyfriend, then walks over to Alexei's bag. As he rifles through it, I stare at my roommate, waiting for him to judge me.

"Is it really the ribs or did Blackwell do something he shouldn't have?"

Well, that's not what I was expecting. I shake my head. "Everything was consensual."

Eli comes back and hands me a bottle. I take it and stare at him. "Apricot oil? I know I'm not exactly an expert here, but how's this supposed to help my ribs?"

Alexei lets out a bark of laughter, the sound startling in the tense quiet of the room. "Is not for injuries, idiot. It's for after."

I stare at him blankly.

Eli huffs out an exasperated breath, his cheeks pinking. "It's for your butthole . . . for when you bottom. Helps with the, uh, soreness and stuff."

Why can't the world swallow me whole when I actually want it to? Seriously, can I just die?

And *butthole*?

But I know fuck all about anal sex, so if this shit helps I'm not turning it down. If only this conversation wasn't happening with me sitting here naked. "Can someone hand me my clothes?"

Alexei grabs my sweats from the floor then kneels and helps get my feet into them.

Motherfucking fuck.

Did Killian fuck me into an alternate reality because these two idiots have turned into Mom and Dad?

Un-fucking-believable.

I grew up in a caring household. I was never abused. Sure, I'm a pure-blooded asshole. Entitled even. My parents are fighters, literally. They met taking kickboxing class. Actually, they met at Crestwood. Think Mom beat the shit out of Dad for something.

But I never had friends care for me the way these two are. Or maybe I just never let anyone.

It's . . . weirdly touching, making my chest tight and this time, it's from more than physical pain.

Eli helps me with the sweatshirt, then smirks. "Guess what they say is true, there's a thin line between love and hate."

"Fuck off, Feisty Mouse. I don't love Killian."

The second the words leave my mouth, something flutters in my stomach and my palms start to sweat. Like Killian said, we're past hate.

But it's not love.

He's just mine or some shit.

"So, why him?"

I roll my eyes. "Because bad decisions make the best stories."

Eli giggles. "Love stories."

That's it. Need to get out of here because if I stay, they'll poke more. And now, different kinds of feelings are bubbling up, ones I'm not ready for.

Not when Alexei flops down beside his boyfriend and wraps his arms around him. I don't need to hold someone the way Alexei holds Eli nor want to be held like that.

Or so I keep telling myself.

But seeing them together, seeing the way they fit like two puzzle pieces sliding into place . . . it makes me wonder, makes me question all the things I thought I knew about myself, about what I need and want and deserve.

It's terrifying. And exhilarating.

But it's a problem for another day.

"Going for a walk." I stand, then slip on my sneakers. "Need to find some Motrin and food."

And it's not a lie. But not entirely the truth.

Between the pain and all the unchecked emotions, I'm suffocating. So, before they can offer to help or stop me, I leave, hoping getting some fresh air will calm the chaos.

Jackson

CHAPTER NINE

I step out of the pharmacy, the small paper bag containing the extra-strength Motrin clutched tightly in my hand. Each movement sends a fresh wave of agony radiating through my chest, and I grit my teeth against the pain, my breath coming in shallow, careful inhales.

The late March air is crisp and biting, and I shiver as I make my way across the parking lot, my steps slow and measured. But I can't let anyone else know I'm hurt this bad. Alexei will keep his mouth shut and he'll control Feisty Mouse.

I wouldn't be the first person to play with broken bones. Guys in the NHL do it all the time. One had a broken wrist throughout the Stanley Cup playoffs. And that body part is needed to score. My ribs, not so much.

Leaning against the side of a building, I struggle to get the childproof cap off. My fingers are clumsy and uncoordinated, and it takes me three tries to get the damn thing open. I shake out four pills, a prescription strength dose, and swallow them dry.

I should probably see a doctor, but I can't risk being benched. This has been my best season yet and I want to finish out strong. Prove to Winnipeg that I'm worth a contract.

Prove it to myself too because Killian's taunts about being a late pick bother me more than I let on.

I just hope the Motrin keeps the agony at bay enough to get through the next few games. Once I'm back in Rosewood Bay my father can have our family doctor prescribe something stronger.

But my hands are tied right now.

Pushing off the concrete wall, I head down the block toward the pizza place. One thing I learned from my mom is not to take ibuprofen on an empty stomach as it causes ulcers.

"Hey."

I grimace at the sound of Killian's voice. Why the fuck is he here and how did he find me?

Closing my eyes and forcing in a deep breath, hoping to hide my pain, I school my features and turn around. "What do you want?"

But taking in the sight of him, I clench my jaw so tight I think my teeth are about to crumble. He looks like hell, his eyes red-rimmed and his golden blonde hair standing up in wild tufts like he's been running his hands through it. His skin is pale, almost ashen, and there's a haunted look in his gaze that makes my chest ache in a way that has nothing to do with my injuries.

"I just wanted to talk, to see what I did wrong?"

Oh, fuck him right now.

"Why are you acting like a dependent fuck? We had sex. We were done. I have shit to do."

Killian flinches like I've slapped him, his eyes widening and glistening. "It was my first time. With a guy. And you . . . I saw your lip tremble, shithead. I hurt you."

Holy Mary, mother of fucks, this man.

"Think you must've come too hard and you're seeing things. I mean, you lost your damn mind with all that 'baby' talk." I shoot him a snarky smile, only it's for show because as much as I hate to admit it, I loved every time the word came out of his mouth.

Killian's face hardens, his eyes flashing with anger and something that looks a lot like disappointment. "For someone who claims it was his first time too, you sure seem to be brushing this off like I'm just another one of your hookups."

"Aren't you though?"

Oh, shit.

Killian glares at me through those thick lashes of his, then grabs my sweatshirt, fisting it and jerking my body forward.

The sudden movement sends a bolt of white-hot agony lancing through my side, and I can't bite back the yelp of pain that tears from my throat. I stumble, my knees buckling, and I grab onto Killian's arms to keep from falling.

He tries to wrap an arm around me, to steady me, but I shove him away, my breath coming in short, panicked gasps. "Don't . . . touch . . ."

"How bad is it?" His voice is dangerously low, and the way he's staring at me, I almost feel like he's going to snap my neck and throw my body in a dumpster. "Jackson, how bad was that hit really?"

My skin tingles, stomach fluttering. For some reason I want to run away. But not because I'm scared of him. It's the fierce protectiveness in his eyes that scares the hell out of me. Because it makes me feel . . . weak.

I take a step back, my shoulders squared and my chin lifted. "What, you planning on using it against me? Think you've got an advantage when we play each other? That is, if you fuckers even make it to the next round."

Killian's face contorts as his hands ball into fists at his sides. "Why do you have to be such a goddamn asshole? I care about you, more than you deserve right this second!"

Something in me snaps, a dam bursting under the weight of too much pressure. I lash out, my fist connecting with Killian's cheek in a clumsy, half-hearted punch.

It's not hard, not really. But it's enough to make my point, to remind him of who we are and what we do.

We fight. It's what feels normal and, right now, I just want to feel normal.

"Hit me." I even stick my chin out. "Come on, Blackwell. You know you want to."

But he doesn't take the bait. Instead, the motherfucker grips my chin so tight I think he might break it.

"Stop calling me Blackwell when we're not on the ice." He growls, his face inches from mine. "And why the fuck did you just punch me?"

"What were you expecting, a kiss hello?"

Something flashes in his eyes, too quick to decipher. "Actually . . ."

And then he's kissing me, his lips soft and warm and insistent against mine. I make a startled sound in the back of my throat, my eyes fluttering closed as his tongue strokes over mine in a way that makes heat pool low in my belly.

It's different from our other kisses, less a battle for dominance and more of a give and take, a sort of push and pull that leaves me breathless and aching, my hands fisting in the front of his shirt to drag him closer.

Killian slides his hand around to cup the back of my neck as he angles his head to deepen it. I let out a moan, embarrassingly needy, and I can feel him smile against my mouth, can feel the way his body relaxes into mine.

He pulls away, leaning his forehead against mine as his thumb strokes over my cheekbone. "So, I did hurt you?"

"Kinda."

"You know, asshole, I was scared I damaged you . . . back there . . . because I honestly had no idea what I was doing. I even searched the internet to see if I was supposed to fuck you differently."

A startled laugh bursts out of me, which I regret immediately as pain lances through my chest. I punch Killian in the arm, scowling at him through watering eyes.

"What was that for?"

"Motherfucker, it hurts to breathe. What do you think it feels like when your dumbass makes me laugh?"

His expression softens, his eyes filled with a tenderness that makes my heart clench. "Can't win with you, can I? So, where are you heading?"

"To get some food. Took some Motrin so I need to get something in my stomach."

He nods, then jerks his head toward the pizzeria, a small smile playing across his full lips. "Let's go. I'm buying."

I raise an eyebrow, a teasing lilt to my voice. "You taking me on a date or some shit?"

Killian smiles wide, his eyes crinkling at the corners, color finally coming back to his cheeks. "What if I am?"

We fall into step beside each other, Killian shooting me concerned glances every few seconds. It should annoy me, should make me feel weak and pathetic.

But it doesn't. Instead, it makes something warm and sweet unfurl in my chest.

"Meant to ask," I say, breaking the comfortable silence, "The first time we fucked around, when I held you down, why'd you freak out?"

"Who said I freaked out?" he asks, his voice carefully neutral.

I roll my eyes. "You went so still it's like someone gave you a paralytic agent."

Killian is quiet for a long moment, his jaw working like he's chewing on his words. "You had your knee on my back. I didn't want you breaking me that way. It wouldn't just take away my career, but also my ability to help my family." He takes a deep breath, his eyes fixed on the ground. "My mom . . . she has muscular dystrophy. And my younger sisters, they're planning on going to college. I feel like it falls on me to take care of them."

While I know I'm an asshole, now I actually feel like one. What's worse is all the regret washing over me for every time I nearly maimed him, even if he's done it to me as well. "Not sure what to say."

He stops walking, turning to face me with an intensity that makes my skin prickle. "Just don't ever use it against me. Call me what you want, demolish my face, but leave my mom out of it."

"You have my word." And I mean it with every fiber of my being. No way will I stand for someone else running their mouth either. Guess this is what he felt like when he saw me get hit—that deep down need to obliterate anyone who might hurt the person I care about. "And . . . the only way I want to destroy that face of yours is with my dick."

Killian barks out a laugh, the tension draining from his shoulders. "All right, shithead. How many slices of pizza can you finish in one sitting?"

I grin, my competitive streak flaring to life. "More than you, fuckface."

"Is that a challenge?"

"Always."

We're laughing as we step into the pizzeria, a permanent shift occurring in our relationship.

Whatever that may be.

Killian

CHAPTER TEN

While I was joking about going to dinner being a date, it actually turned into one. Jackson and I sat there talking, like normal people. Well, almost normal, since we constantly threw out challenges to each other, from who could eat more to who could finish their soda the fastest to who could shove the most food into their mouth at once, even throwing in the occasional insult and tons of curses.

But that's just us.

Even better is that instead of fighting, we ended up laughing. Okay, not better since he ended up in pain. It's just nice to see we have a connection.

"Told you to fucking run." He growls the moment we step into the lobby.

After we left, Jackson started teasing about hunting me. But it became more serious the closer we got to the hotel, his eyes changing to dark and hungry.

I let out a long-suffering sigh, trying to ignore the way my cock twitches in my jeans. "Chasing after me is the last thing you should be doing right now."

He just shoves his keycard into my palm, then gives me a rough push, his lip curling up into a snarl that sends heat rushing south.

"Run." The word is a deep, guttural command, his eyes flashing with primal need.

I swallow hard, adjusting myself as subtly as I can. This is a bad idea. He's in no condition to be exerting himself like this, even if the Motrin alleviated some of his pain. But the wanton desperation in his gaze, the raw desire . . . it calls to something deep inside, something wild and reckless and so damn eager to submit to.

So I turn on my heel and take off, my heart hammering against my ribs as his footsteps pound behind me.

God, what is it about being hunted by Jackson that gets me so hot? It shouldn't turn me on like this, shouldn't make my blood sing with adrenaline *and* arousal. But the thought of him catching me, claiming me, marking me as his . . . it's the most intoxicating thing I've ever felt.

I risk a glance over my shoulder and nearly stumble at the intensity in his eyes, the predatory curl of his lips. He looks like a man possessed, like a rabid beast ready to devour me whole.

And fuck, do I love it.

I slow my pace just a fraction, letting him gain ground as we round the corner toward the elevators. They're so tantalizingly close, but I know better than to wait for one.

Instead, I burst through the door to the stairwell and take the steps two at a time.

One more dumb move considering my team has another game to play.

By the time I reach Jackson's floor, my lungs are screaming for air and my skin is slick with sweat. I burst through the door, expecting to have a few seconds' head start ... But he's already there, lounging against the wall like he hasn't just sprinted up six flights. The bastard must've caught the elevator, the one I foolishly bypassed.

He smirks at me, giving a mocking little wave before launching himself forward. I fumble with the keycard, but by some miracle it works on the first try. I fling the door open and dart inside, leaving it wide for him to follow.

The moment the door slams shut behind us, Jackson is on me. His hands fist my sweatshirt while mine coil into his thick chestnut hair as our mouths crash together. The kiss is brutal, all teeth and tongue and desperate hunger. He bites at my lips even as his fingers work at the fly of my jeans, his movements rough and graceless.

"You slowed down, fuckface," he rasps, nipping at my jaw. "You'll pay for that."

I groan, my own hands scrabbling at his clothes with far more finesse. "I want to feel you inside me, asshole. Not ride in the back of an ambulance because you pushed too hard."

He grabs my cock through my boxers, squeezing hard enough to make me see stars. "Damn, Kill. You really like being hunted. Look how much you're leaking."

I can't help the needy whine that escapes me, my hips bucking into his touch. He's right, I'm already shamefully wet, the fabric of my underwear clinging obscenely to the head of my dick.

"Moaning like a starved slut already?" He chuckles darkly, his hand working me with ruthless efficiency. "So desperate for me. Don't worry, I remember the way you fucked me. Time to return the favor. Make you my bitch."

The filthy words send a bolt of pure want straight to my cock, and I damn near come on the spot. I've never been so turned on in my life, never felt so utterly consumed by need.

"Strip and get on the bed, face down, and put that gorgeous ass I'm about to wreck up in the air."

I scramble to obey, nearly tripping over my feet in my haste to shed my clothes. By the time I'm naked and positioned on the bed, my chest pressed to the mattress and my ass hitched high, I'm shaking and my cock hangs heavy between my legs, dripping steadily onto the sheets.

The crinkle of a pharmacy bag draws my attention, and I glance back to see Jackson rummaging through it before tossing it aside, a bottle of lube and some condoms in his hand. He drops them on the bed beside me, his eyes glinting with dark promise.

"Time to teach you not to treat me with care. Remind you I'm a fucking Titan, injured or not." His palm cracks across my ass without warning, hard and unforgiving.

I grunt and look over my shoulder just as the next strike lands. "What the fu—"

"Face forward before I use my belt."

I blink at least fifty times. Or so I think. It's a lot because I'm having difficulty processing what he just said. When I don't move, he lands another searing smack to my rear, the pain of it zinging straight to my cock.

"You want the belt, Kill?"

Do I?

I swallow hard, my mouth gone dry. The thought of it, of being at his mercy like that . . . my body trembles.

"I'm . . . curious," I say, the words a little more than a croak.

His grin is sharp and wicked, his eyes gleaming with sadistic delight. "I've used it on girls before so I know what I'm doing. Just tell me to stop if it's not for you."

Something hot and ugly rears its head in my chest, my vision flashing red at the thought of him with someone else, of his hands, his lips, his body bringing pleasure to anyone but me. "Go near another pussy or cock and I'll rip that person's head off and put their skull on a pike outside your dorm."

His mouth falls open, eyes widening for a brief second before a full-on smile spreads across his face. "That is the most threatening way I've ever been made happy. You know, maybe I should—"

"Try me, motherfucker."

He snickers, staring right into my eyes. "You could just ask to be my boyfriend, asshole."

My mouth opens and closes but no words come out. Is that what I want? Jackson's the second person to mention it.

But I don't have time to dwell on it, because Jackson pulls away then crosses the room to rifle through his suitcase. When he comes back, there's a leather belt dangling from his fist, silver buckle gleaming in the low light.

My cock jerks at the sight, a fresh bead of precum welling at the tip. Jackson notices, of course he does, and his grin turns feral.

"I'd say you're more than a little curious, Kill." He trails the smooth leather over the curve of my ass. "That's a steady stream you're drooling there. Fucking slut for it already, aren't you?"

I can only whimper, my back arching as much as it can, my ass in the air as an offering. I've never been so turned on, so desperate to be used.

Holding the buckle in the palm of his hand, he pulls back his arm halfway before letting it fly. The leather wraps around the swell of my cheeks with a delicious, searing bolt of pain.

"Fuck!" My fingers scramble at the sheets as he rains down blow after blow, layering the hurt until my entire world narrows to the white-hot sting of it. "Oh, God."

He works me over with brutal efficiency, the belt licking fire across my skin until I'm writhing and reduced to nothing but sensation. The pain and the pleasure mixing together, feeding off each other until I'm drunk with it, mindless and pliant.

"Jackson," I choke out, my voice cracking on a moan. "Please..."

"Keep saying my name like that." He tosses the belt aside to grip my reddened cheeks with greedy hands. "And I'll fuck you till you scream it."

He spreads me open, baring my hole to his hungry gaze. I feel exposed, vulnerable in a way I never have before. But God, the heat of his breath ghosting over my sensitive skin . . . it makes me shake and clench, makes me want in a way I can't even name.

"Look at you," he murmurs, trailing a finger over my twitching rim. "So pretty here, all pink and untouched. Fucking mouthwatering. I wanna taste you, Kill. Wanna see how deep I can get my tongue into this tight little hole."

I keen high in my throat, my hips canting back in shameless offering. "Please. Please, I need it. I need you. Please just—"

The first swipe of his tongue punches the air from my lungs, my eyes rolling back in my head at the slick, filthy sensation. He licks over my hole again and again, laving and sucking and stroking until I'm a babbling, incoherent mess.

"You taste and smell like heaven." He points his tongue, then pushes inside, breaching me with velvety, wet heat, and I nearly fly out of my skin.

It's too much yet not enough all at once, a pleasure so intense it borders on pain.

"Jackson. Oh, fuck. Don't stop. Fuck fuck fuck—"

He growls against me, the vibrations making me clench and shudder. He grips my cheeks hard and spreads them wider, fucking his tongue deeper, harder, sloppy and obscene.

"Ride my face. Take what you need."

I sob and rock back onto him, letting him hold me open and plunder me with single-minded focus. Every stroke of his tongue lights me up from the inside, stoking the fire in my gut until I'm sure I'll combust with the force of it.

He rakes his teeth over my hole, sucking at it before diving inside once more, following that up by a sharp smack that makes my legs shake. "Need to fill you until you drip with my cum. You're mine, Killian. I want everyone knowing how thoroughly I fucked you. I want them to smell it on you."

He pulls away, my hole clenching around nothing. I crane my neck to look back at him, a needy whine escaping my throat at the sight that greets me.

He's standing at the foot of the bed, slowly undressing. My gaze roams over his body, drinking in every detail—the defined ridges of his abs, the broad expanse of his chest, the powerful curves of his biceps, and those thick, muscular thighs.

But it's the marks I've left that make my breath catch. The bruises and scratches, the imprints of my teeth on his skin. Proof that he's mine, that I've claimed him.

When my eyes finally drift lower, to the hard, flushed jut of his cock, I can't bite back the moan that rises in my throat. Jackson smirks, slow and filthy as he reaches for the bottle of lube, slicking his fingers with deliberate, obscene motions. "Don't worry. I'm gonna give this needy hole what it wants. Gonna stuff you full and make you mine."

Two slicked up fingers force their way inside my body and I yell, so worked up I can't contain it even if I wanted, which I don't. He pumps into me hard and fast, crooking his fingers just right to nail my prostate with every thrust.

"Please, Jackson, I can't . . . I need. . ."

Jackson chuckles, then sinks his teeth into the tender flesh of my ass, biting down and sucking hard enough to leave a bruise. "This is mine. It belongs to me."

He does it again on the other cheek and I clench around his fingers as he works me open, stretching and scissoring until I'm loose and wet and aching for more.

I look back at him when he withdraws his fingers, my mouth opening to say . . . something, anything. But the words stick in my throat as I catch the furrow of his brows, the tightness around his eyes. The barely-there flinch as he shifts his weight, his ribs no doubt screaming in protest.

"Jackson—"

"Shut it." He slides his hard cock between my ass cheeks, slicking it up with the lube and saliva already there. "I need this."

I do to. All of it.

So when he twists to pick up the condoms, I smack them off the bed. "Take me, Jackson. All of me."

"You sure?"

I nod.

With a low, rumbling growl, he drives forward, breaching me in one long, relentless stroke and I swear I feel it in my fucking soul. It hurts, the stretch and burn almost too much to take.

"God, fuck, Kill. So good. Perfect fit for me. My cock belongs inside you."

He grips the back of my neck, pinning me down as he ruts into me, not waiting for me to adjust. Each thrust of his hips rocks me forward on the bed. Tears spring to my eyes, blurring my vision, but I don't care.

Because he's fucking me like the brutal Titan he is, owning me, staking his claim.

I can't stop the broken noises that spill from my lips, the choked-off sobs and wordless pleas as I push back to meet his thrusts, my hips rolling in desperate little figure eights, trying to pull him deeper.

"That's it. Ride my dick. Ride it like it belongs to you because it does."

He wraps a hand around my aching length and jerks me in time with his targeted thrusts until it feels like a spring tightening inside me. "Harder. Oh, fuck. Harder, please."

His fist tugs at my piercings in a way that makes my eyes roll back. My body erratically pushes back into him before thrusting forward into his hand over and over until I'm a sweaty, writhing mess.

"Look at you riding my dick like a fucking king. Come on it, Killian. Show me how much you need it, how desperate you are for me to fill this sweet hole."

I shatter with a hoarse cry, my orgasm ripping through me like a freight train. Jackson fucks me through it, milking every drop from my cock as I spill over his fist and onto the sheets.

He leans over me, hips working in short, frantic bursts, and sinks his teeth into the back of my neck as he buries himself to the hilt.

I feel the hot rush of his release, the twitch and pulse of his cock as he empties himself inside me. It seems to go on forever, each feral grunt and snarl sending aftershocks racing down my spine.

Finally, he collapses on top of me, his breath gusting hot and damp against my ear. We lay like that for long minutes, trembling and gasping, our sweat-slick skin sticking together.

When he pulls out, I can't bite back my whimper at the loss. He rolls to the side with a groan, flopping onto his back, and I realize for the first time how pale he is beneath his flush.

"You were right. I shouldn't have—"

"No shit," I snap, taking in his still paling complexion. I want to smack him, punch him, knock some sense into him. "You're not fucking invincible, Jackson."

"Says who?" He reaches for my hand, then laces our fingers together. "Besides, it was worth it."

I roll my eyes as I get off the bed. My ass throbs with every movement, the skin hot and tender, but it's a good ache. In the bathroom, I clean myself up, even pushing some of his cum back inside me.

Then I grab a washcloth and bring it back to the bed. Jackson watches me through heavy-lidded eyes as I wipe the sweat and lube from his skin. I sort of like taking care of him. I mean, it's just post sex cleanup. But I feel . . . needed by him. "About your earlier comment, I think I'd like that."

He quirks a brow, a slow smile tugging at his lips. "And which comment would that be?"

"You know which one, asshole."

"Falling in love with me already?" He bats his eyes and plasters on a big grin.

"Maybe." Figured my response would shut him up, throw him off. Bet he figured I'd backpedal.

What I don't expect is for his cheeks to turn bright red as he smiles so wide, as if I've just handed him the moon. It does something to my insides, and when he lifts up onto his elbows and kisses me, I'm done for.

"Killian Blackwell, like you ever had a choice in being anything other than mine."

I give him the finger. "You're such a cocky bastard. And by the way, my mom already called you *my* boyfriend anyway, which means I'm not yours. You're *mine*."

His eyes widen, mouth fully agape. "You told your mom about me?"

"Uh, yeah. She wants to meet you."

"You're going to kill me," he mumbles, pulling me back into bed, his hands sliding down to grab my ass, possessive and sure, and the ache of it makes me shiver. "I hope you know that."

I grin, nipping at his bottom lip. "Well, yeah. It's been written in the stars since the day we were probably born. Definitely since the day I kicked your ass at camp back when we were ten."

"In your dreams, fuckface. Everyone knows I won that fight." He looks down at my neck. "Your teammates ask about the bruising?"

"Not outright." Raiyne's been the most curious, especially since I've been disappearing.

Trembley too.

Both of them have made passing comments about me hooking up with an aggressive girl, and I haven't bothered to correct them. Not that it's about being a guy. It's just because it's *Jackson*.

It certainly doesn't help that we're playing against each other tomorrow. The winner will move on to the semi-finals. The loser's season comes to an end. And I won't be taking it easy on the asshole.

It's not who we are.

But once playoffs are over, I don't have to hide who I've fallen in love with. I'm not sure how my friends will feel about it, but maybe it won't be such a big deal if we win.

Either way, I'll come out winning something, and I can't help but be happy about it.

"Between the two of us, we've given each other more bruises in the past few days than in the years we spent fighting. Guess we've always been marking one another, just never realized it."

Jackson playfully punches me in the dick. "Like you said, asshole, it was written in the stars."

Killian

CHAPTER ELEVEN

The roar of the crowd engulfs me as I line up for the opening faceoff. Across from me, Jackson crouches low, his eyes locked on mine with breath-stealing intensity. Our sticks hover mere inches apart, the anticipation crackling between us like electricity.

I still can't believe how stubborn he is, how determined to play through the pain. He's going to push himself to the limit, and he's going to push me right along with him.

Can't say I wouldn't do the same.

The ref drops the puck and our sticks clash in a flurry. I gain inside leverage on Jackson, angling my hip to nudge him off balance. The puck skips free toward my winger but Jackson recovers, his hand darting out to tug at my jersey as he gives chase.

"Asshole." I bat his hand away.

He just smirks, then slams his hip into mine, sending me crashing into the boards. "Not getting through me that easy."

I grit my teeth and push off the boards, my skates carving deep grooves into the ice as I race after him. We battle for the loose puck, our bodies colliding and tangling in a dance that's as familiar as breathing. I absorb his shoves and sweep the puck away, evading his next attempt at a check.

The Titans' defense stack up at their blue line, only, I'm not giving up that easily. But Jackson slams into me from the side, pinning me up against the glass with the full weight of his body. "Where do you think you're going?"

"To win this fucking game."

My team moves the puck around with quick, precise passes. Trembley takes a slap shot but Novotny blocks it, his pads absorbing the impact with a dull thud.

I lunge for the rebound, my stick outstretched, but Zach Knight beats me there, sending the puck skittering up the boards and out of reach. Jackson scoops it up, then passes to Walsh, the two of them tearing off down the ice like bullets.

I curse under my breath and pivot to give chase, my lungs burning with the effort. Luckily, our goalie comes through with a glove save and I skate off to the bench.

We trade more cheap shots and hits as the period ends scoreless.

Much of the second period is the same. Scoreless. Cheap shots. Mostly legal hitting.

It's not like our normal games. Can't be. These refs won't allow it, and they're the ones in control.

I sprint back to break up a two-on-one chance. As I pivot to chase the puck up the ice, my winger banks it off the boards in a perfect pass. I stretch out my stick to receive it, my eyes locked on the prize, but my feet fly out from under me.

"Oops, sorry about that." Jackson's smirk is back as he scoops up the turnover.

I grind my teeth. Part of me wishes I didn't know about his ribs because I'd lay the fucker out right here, right now.

Petrov takes a slapshot and it goes off our goalie's stick and out of bounds. As Jackson skates by, I glare at him for the trip. "Listen, fuckface. Don't think I won't get back at you."

He just grins, cocky and infuriating. "What are you going to do?"

I skate closer, keeping an eye on the refs and our teammates as I lean in, making sure to look like I'm goading him. "Maybe drug your ass and lock your cock in a chastity cage while you're knocked out. Won't let you out for a week."

He jerks, his eyes wide and shocked. "You . . . We're in the middle of a game. You can't say that shit right now."

I chuckle and skate away. Good to know sex talk will throw my boyfriend off kilter.

But my triumph is short-lived. On our next shift, Jackson's on breakaway, Trembley hot on his heels, only Jackson's faster, his skates flashing as he dekes and spins, slipping the puck through our goalie's five-hole like it's nothing.

"Dammit!"

He shoots me the finger and the biggest shit-eating grin the asshole's yet to give.

Raiyne comes over and bumps my shoulder. "Next goal is mine. No way are we losing."

The next face-off, our team turns it up a notch. We play more brutal, use our bodies more. The Titans respond in kind, but one of their rookie defensemen makes a critical error, tangling with Novotny, allowing for Raiyne to slip one in with a wraparound.

Two shifts later, Jackson flies down the ice, his skates eating up the distance as he weaves through our defenders like they're standing still. He fakes out our goalie with a dizzying series of dekes, then goes top-shelf with a wrist shot that leaves us all stunned.

I slam my stick on the ice, then freeze when Trembley doesn't slow down and barrels into Jackson with a vicious, late hit, the sound of their bodies colliding, echoing through the rink like a gunshot.

Jackson cries out as he crumples to the ice, his stick clattering uselessly beside him. For a moment, the world seems to slow, the roar of the crowd fading to a distant buzz in my ears. All I can see is Jackson, curled in on himself, his face twisted in agony.

I'm moving before I can even think, my skates carrying me across the ice in a wild, reckless charge. I shove Trembley from behind, sending him flying with the force of my fury. "You stupid fuck!"

Trembley whirls around to face me. "What the hell, Blackwell!"

I grab his jersey and swing, then swing again over and over, my gloved hand connecting with his helmet each time. "Hurt what's mine again and see what happens. I dare you."

My teammates pull us apart and Raiyne shoves me away from everyone. My chest heaves and I look away from his judgmental gaze, my own falling to Jackson still on the ice. The refs call over the Titans' trainer, sending us all back to our benches.

I want to go to him, want to shove every one of them aside and gather him up in my arms. But I can't.

Finally, they help Jackson to his feet, his arm slung over Petrov's shoulder as he's helped off the ice. My jaw clenches, nostrils flaring. I want to follow, to go to him. But right now, my own team looks like they're out for my blood.

Trembley gets handed a major penalty, and Coach benches me for the rest of the period. I just sit there, not saying a word, my hands shaking and my mind reeling.

"So, he's *yours*?" Raiyne's tone is both curious and angry. "That's who you've been hiding out with lately?"

I nod.

"And what, we're all supposed to just roll over for them now? Let them win because you're fucking their center?"

His words hit me like a punch to the gut and I jerk back, then turn and look at him. "I wasn't taking it easy on him or any of them. Don't question why I'm here."

"Blackwell, keep your fucking mouth shut," Coach hisses.

My fists clench, nails digging into my palms. Everyone is busy being pissed off at me, when all I want to know is if the man I'm in love with is okay.

Jackson

CHAPTER TWELVE

Nothing like having to come to practice only to sit in the stands as the rest of the team runs drills to get ready for the Frozen Four. It's like pouring lemon juice on a papercut. At least we ended up winning against the Serpents but only by one point.

What makes it worse is now I can't pretend, can't fake that I'm better because the diagnosis is official. Multiple rib fractures. So, I'm out the rest of the post season. I don't get to play in the biggest game of the year.

I pull out my phone to check for any messages from Killian before entering the locker room. He has a meeting with his coach. Can't say anyone was happy finding out about our relationship.

Okay, that's not true.

My parents were all right with it, though they would've much preferred meeting my boyfriend under different circumstances than at the hospital. Mom finds it hysterical we've beaten the shit out of each other.

But Killian's team's been icing him out. Not all of them. Though, they all did make it a point to be clear it wasn't about his sexuality, that it was about *me*.

Like I didn't see that coming.

I tuck my phone back into my pocket since there are no new messages, and with a long sigh enter the locker room.

Viktor's glaring, still pissed that Alexei and Eli knew about my sexy times with Killian and he was kept in the dark. Knight and Walsh, on the other hand, were angry at first because they thought I was taking it light on Killian during the game.

Then Eli had to blabber how I'd known something was wrong with my ribs from the Cornell game. Now they're mad at me for hiding an injury *and* letting the Cornell asshole get away unscathed.

Petrov scoots over and I grit my teeth against the flare of pain as I ease myself onto the bench. "Eli's bringing dinner later. Wants to know if Blackwell is stopping by."

"Not sure. Haven't heard from him yet."

Viktor whistles. "Your boy toy's in trouble, huh? Can't help that we knocked them out of contention."

I just wave him off, then turn to Walsh and Knight, the latter of which just grabs his stick and walks out of the locker room. He's still pissed at me. Walsh, however, nods in my direction. "How you holding up?"

"I'll live. Just sucks missing out on the big game."

Viktor throws a wadded ball of used tape at me. "We'll win it just for you, then you can tell me who the bottom is."

I roll my eyes when he waggles his brows. The idiot has been bothering me to find out who to add to his little chat group since the game.

"You'll be out there next year." Walsh taps my foot with his stick before heading to the ice.

I watch each of them go until the locker room is empty. I want to be out there with them, want to feel the burn of my muscles as I push myself to the limit. Want to taste victory.

But I can't. And it's killing me, bit by bit.

I sit back and rest my head on the wall, closing my eyes as I linger for a bit, not ready to head out and sit in the stands just yet. I pull my phone out to check it again, hoping for a distraction from the dark spiral of my thoughts.

"Reed."

Assistant Coach Buckland stands in front of the closed door. There's something in his expression that sets me on edge, more so than usual.

"Coach Nieminen already chewed me out about hiding the injury, don't need to hear—"

"Shut the fuck up. We both know you're using your ribs as an excuse to cover for taking it easy on your little boyfriend." He spits the last word like its poison, his lip curling.

I stand, my hands balling into fists. "You don't know what the fuck you're talking about."

Buckland scoffs, stalking closer to get right up in my face. "Don't I? Between you and Petrov, seems like sticking your dicks into ass effectively neutered the both of you. Or do you two faggots take it in the ass?"

I bare my teeth, dropping my phone to take a swing at his head, but he weaves, then his fist collides with my already battered ribs, the pain so intense, it sends me crashing to my knees.

"What's wrong? Does it hurt too much?" He spits on me, then laughs. "If I'd known I'd be coaching a team full of cocksuckers, I never would have taken it."

"My father will never—"

"You think I'm scared of your daddy? No, he got me this job because he owed my family a favor. Yeah, that's right. Dear old dad *owed us* a favor."

"Fuck you." I try to stand, only he throws a kick to my upper body that knocks me back down. "What are you even talking about?"

Buckland's face twists into an ugly sneer. "A few years ago, your dad falsely accused my sister of stealing from his precious company. She was one of his accountants. She went to jail for three years, all because he didn't look further into the situation. Believed one of his *friends*, the real culprit. And when she finally got out, when the truth came out and she was exonerated? It was too late. She was never the same, never fully recovered."

I close my eyes, trying to catch my breath. But every inhale sends pain shooting through me like shards of glass filling my lungs. Still, I try to remember back. Sure, there were times things were tense at home because of work. Nothing more than usual.

"She tried to kill herself," he whispers, his voice thick with a twisted sort of glee. "Slit her wrists in the bathtub. And you're just like him, another entitled prick who thinks he can do whatever he wants without consequences. Well, guess what? Your free ride ends now."

He punctuates each word with a kick to my body. I try to crawl away, to shield myself from the onslaught, but he's relentless.

Merciless.

And he just keeps hitting me, keeps kicking me. I curl in on myself, my arms wrapped around my head, praying for it to end.

"You cost me a lot of money, you little shit. Had a big bet riding on that game." He grabs my hair, yanking my head up. "Does your old man know he raised a fucking queer?"

My chest crackles with every breath, the fractures no doubt full breaks now. But I'm not going down without a fight. Fuck him and his misplaced blame and his thirst for vengeance.

I swing my arm, my fist connecting with his cheek. "You homophobic piece of shit."

His head snaps to the side, a look of shock and fury crossing his features. But it's short-lived. Before I can even blink, his knuckles split my lip, filling my mouth with the coppery tang of fresh blood.

He stands, looming over me. "You and your friends think you run this team. Delusional pieces of shit. Doesn't matter how much money you have—someone will always get to you if they really want to."

His foot connects with my face in a burst of blinding pain, stars exploding behind my eyelids. "Now your father will know what it felt like for my family. He'll know what it's like to watch someone you love suffer."

As the darkness closes in and the pain swallows me whole, my last thought is of Killian and those honey-brown eyes. And how I'll never get to tell him how I feel.

That I . . . love him.

Killian

CHAPTER THIRTEEN

Not hearing from Jackson just adds insult to injury. Coach reamed me out for my *extracurricular* activities during Regionals, especially with the enemy. Luckily, video replay showed I hadn't been playing any differently than I normally do.

But going after my teammate was a hard line for him.

Trembley crashed the meeting to forgive me in front of our coach, making me feel even more like shit. Outside of a verbal ass whooping, nothing really happened. Our season is over, and they can't kick me off the team because of who I choose to date.

Most likely, I won't be captain next year, but I'm okay with that in more ways than one. Seriously, babysitting the Serpents' hunts is exhausting. I'll gladly hand over the reins to someone else.

"Fuck!" I look up at the sky. "Universe, please don't let them punish me by making me captain again."

"Blackwell."

I whip my head to the left, the thick Russian accent too familiar to ignore. Alexei Petrov leans against a creamy silver Mercedes G-wagon.

"What are you doing here?"

He pulls the backdoor open. "Get in."

"Uh, yeah. No thank you."

My heart plummets when Viktor Novotny gets out of the passenger side. "Get in the fucking car. Now."

Slowly walking forward, I look inside, but Jackson's not in there. When I freeze up, Petrov grabs my nape and shoves me in. I fall face first onto the seat and try to turn around to get back out but his large frame is there.

"What the fuck! What are you two doing?"

Novotny gets back into the SUV and closes the door. "Need to talk . . . and take care of something."

Petrov rounds the vehicle, then gets in. He mumbles something in Russian and pulls away from the curb. I take out my phone and text Jackson to figure out what the fuck is going on.

"He won't answer."

"Why?"

I nearly vomit at the sorrowful look on Novotny's face. The Titans' goalie is unhinged, like a crazy fucking clown. But sad—I've never seen this expression on him before—the tension in the air only makes it worse.

"What happened?"

Petrov goes to speak but Novotny cuts him off. "Our assistant coach has an issue with *us gays* as he likes to say just low enough for me to hear. Most of the time, it's just disgusted looks, or the occasional comment directed at me."

"Fucker's too much of a pussy to say it to my face." Petrov sneers, venom lacing his tone.

Novotny looks me dead in the eye. "He beat the fuck out of Jackson. We found him passed out on the floor in the locker room. "

"Pull over!" My hand covers my mouth. "Now!"

The SUV barely comes to a stop before I fling the door open and puke.

No. No. No.

Of all the reasons I thought Jackson didn't answer me, this wasn't one of them. I empty my stomach once more, then wipe my mouth, fighting back the tears. "Where is he?"

"Stonybrook." Novotny claps a hand on my shoulder. "But we have something to take care of right now, so pull it the fuck together."

I straighten to my full height. "No, we need to go to—"

"After. Right now, there's a more pressing issue." His ice blue eyes narrow. "Or was Jackson just for funsies?"

I step into his space, then fist his shirt. "Say something stupid like that again and I'll throw your ass right into oncoming traffic."

He laughs, the sound disturbingly musical. "Then get in and stop making us late."

Releasing his shirt, I get back in, and we pull back onto the highway.

About forty-five minutes later, we roll into the parking lot of Sunset Harbor Marina. Petrov drives to the end, and we walk to a slip where a sixty-nine-foot Galeon is docked. Walsh and Knight are on board along with Mr. Reed.

Why are they on the South Shore?

Jackson's father gives me a curt nod as I board, then heads up a flight of stairs to the second deck. A few minutes later, boat pulls out.

"Anyone care to tell me what we're doing?"

The four of them look at me as if I should know, but all I can think about right now is Jackson, and the fact his father is here with us, so this must be important.

"Our former stupid cunt of a coach is inside. He's about to meet his maker." Walsh takes a sip of whatever's in his tumbler. "And since you're Jackson's boyfriend we figured you'd want in."

"I'm in."

Knight sits next to Walsh in the huge U-shaped dinette area, his own drink in hand. He swirls the glass, then looks out at the horizon as if he's just on a cruise instead of about to commit murder.

Petrov and Novotny disappear to the bar, talking in Russian as they walk away. Great so now it's me, the psycho, and the ruthless snob. Outside of Jackson—and hockey—none of us have a thing in common.

"Is he okay?"

"He'll live," Knight says with no emotion, almost as a matter of fact. He looks me up and down, as if assessing me, or scanning me. Like, is he a real person or some advanced robot these rich fucks might have access to? "You just going to stand there like a dumbass?"

"Fuck off."

Walsh gulps down his drink and sets the tumbler down. "You two are boring me, but he's right, Killian. It's not a quick ride. Might as well take a seat. We don't . . . Yeah, we totally bite. But we kicked your ass right out of the playoffs, so we're cool for tonight."

"Gee, thanks."

When the water gets a bit choppy, I do finally sit but on one of the stools near the large aft galley. Restless energy courses through me. This guy is on the boat. He hurt Jackson. Enough that Mr. Reed is even partaking in whatever is about to happen.

The knot in my stomach grows. It has to be bad.

About thirty minutes later the Galeon slows down. Another smaller boat is in front of us. The people on board wave, then appear to start tidying up. Someone empties a pail into the water and I spot a fin.

Chum.

When the smaller boat leaves, the engine of the Galeon stops. The yacht rocks on the water, adding to my already queasy stomach. Petrov and Novotny reappear with the Titan's assistant coach, and I recognize the fucker from our games.

The man's face is already swollen, bruised, and bleeding. Seeing him, gagged, arms tied behind him, nearly sends me into a frenzy. Everything pulsates as if each cell is beating in time with my heart. Even my ears are ringing.

Mr. Reed comes down, his black suit impeccable, hair slicked back. He shoves the assistant coach to the floor and kicks him in the face. The man falls onto his back, groaning, but his eyes narrow, full of pure hatred.

I'd be scared to death if I was in that position, and it pisses me off he isn't, as if he has no regret for what he did, no fear of the consequences.

Petrov reaches down and lifts the man by his collar off the ground to his feet and drags him over to the stern platform. "Time's almost up."

Knight appears by my side and holds out a knife. "We had our fun already. Your turn. Just don't kill him."

"And don't make him bleed too much. I want him conscious as he's eaten alive," Mr. Reed says, his tone menacing.

Now I get it. The chum. The fins. They're sharks. And this homophobic fuck is about to be their dinner.

My hands are shaking as I take the knife but not from fear. I'll have no regrets once I'm done. Petrov and Walsh hold the motherfucker as I step forward, tightly gripping the hilt. Each breath comes out ragged, yet I do my best to stay calm even though I want to gut this fuck.

I look right into his eyes as I slice his cheek, deciding to keep all my cuts to his face. "Jackson's mine, and you tried to take him from me."

Another slice across his other cheek. "But you failed. He's tougher, stronger than you'll ever be, you piece of shit."

One slice across his forehead.

"You won't get a chance to try again or hurt another person."

This time I buck-fifty his face on both sides from the corners of his mouth to his ears.

Mr. Reed places a hand on my shoulder and squeezes, pulling me back until he's standing in front of the assistant coach. Walsh takes the gag off and the man spits in Mr. Reed's face. "Too bad that faggot son of yours is still breathing. You ruined my sister, my family."

Jackson's father remains calm, wiping the saliva from his cheek as if it were just a speck of dirt. "I will always carry the guilt of what happened with your sister. But my son . . . You're a fucking pussy. You should've come after me."

The man sneers. "I did, only you were too stupid to figure it out."

"No one, for any reason, touches my family." Mr. Reed looks the man dead in his eyes. "And just so you know, God's out to lunch so scream, bitch."

He push-kicks the guy overboard.

It doesn't take long for the screaming to start. With his hands still bound, he can't even try to get back on board. Two fins breach the water and the next second the asshole gets dragged under, then resurfaces.

It's a feeding frenzy.

We all watch the motherfucker until the screams stop and he gets dragged under for good. Everyone's face is a blanket of calm coldness. Not sure if mine is, especially since I'm a bundle of nerves, needing to get to Jackson.

But the rest of them—Jackson's father included—look like regal, ruthless, stone-cold kings.

Mr. Reed turns to me. "Let this be a warning. Hurt my son and you're next."

"Should we just push him over now?" We all stare at Novotny, who only shrugs. "Well, they beat each other up constantly, and you said—"

"Shut it, you idiot." Alexei slaps his cousin upside the head.

I look back to Jackson's father. "I'd burn the goddamn world to make sure there isn't another soul who thinks they can hurt him."

Petrov laughs. "You know, you're sounding more and more like a Titan."

Ignoring him, my shoulders sag as I stare at Jackson's father, my bottom lip trembling. "Can I go see Jackson now? Please?"

His father nods, then returns to the top deck. Moments later, we're heading back to the marina. Can't say we're calm, but we're all definitely quiet. Even Novotny.

And it scares the shit out of me because I don't know exactly what I'm walking into.

Jackson

CHAPTER FOURTEEN

The incessant beeping of the heart monitor drags me from the depths of unconsciousness, each high-pitched tone sending a spike of pain through my skull. I try to lift my arm to grab the damn thing and rip it from the wall. But my limbs may as well be made of lead, heavy and uncooperative. The antiseptic smell of the hospital room invades my nostrils, making my stomach churn and my head spin even more.

I crack my eyes open, just a sliver, and the fluorescent lights above stab into my retinas like knives, forcing me to slam them shut again with a groan. I take a few deep breaths, trying to will away the throbbing in my temples before slowly blinking and letting my vision adjust to the harsh brightness.

The ceiling tiles swim into focus above me, their ugly ass generic white pattern blurring and shifting. Seriously, I need to get out of this depressing room with its stark white walls and beeping machines. It's like being trapped in a fucking sci-fi movie.

Someone's holding my hand tightly, their warmth seeping into my skin. I assume it's my mother until I turn my head toward the figure slumping in the uncomfortable-looking chair beside my bed.

Killian.

His golden blonde hair is a mess, sticking up in every direction, and his clothes are rumpled and creased. His jaw is covered in stubble, and his eyes are underlined with dark circles.

He looks wrecked, exhausted, but still so fucking beautiful it makes my heart ache.

"Hey, you," I rasp, my voice sounding like I've been gargling glass. My throat is raw and scratchy, each word sending a fresh wave of pain through my esophagus.

Killian's eyes flutter open, and he sits up straighter, his grip on my hand tightening until it's almost painful. "You're up."

"No, this is all a dream, or a dream within a dream." I start to laugh, but the movement sends shockwaves of agony through my battered body, and I end up groaning instead.

"Always gotta be an asshole, huh?" Killian's lips twitch into a small smile, but it doesn't reach his eyes as he leans closer, his thumb stroking over the back of my hand.

"But you love me anyway." The words slip out before I can stop them, and I freeze, my heart monitor picking up speed as I wait for his response.

Killian just smiles, soft and tender, then brings my hand up to his lips, pressing a gentle kiss to my knuckles. "Yeah, I do. God help me, but I really fucking do."

The moment is broken by the slight scrape of a chair against the linoleum floor, and I tear my gaze away from Killian to my dad, who rises from his seat in the corner of the room. A tired smile creases his face, and his normally impeccable suit is wrinkled.

My mother dozes, curled on a small couch near the window.

Yesterday was long, a blur of pain and confusion. I barely remember it, but at some point, detectives came to my room to ask questions. Before they entered, Mom gave me the subtle warning to watch what I say. In other words, my father was taking care of shit. She also mentioned the Titans were helping him.

No surprise there. My friends always have my back.

Luckily, the detectives didn't stay long. It helped that between the concussion and all the pain, it was hard for me to recall details.

Dad stands on the other side of my bed, offering me a weak smile and looking ten years older than his actual age. "How're you feeling?"

"Like shit." I close my eyes for a second, taking a few shallow breaths. Every inch of my body hurts, from my toes to the roots of my hair. "When can I get the hell out of here?"

"Not for another day or two." Dad's voice is firm, leaving no room for argument. "And don't even ask me to pull strings. Your mother put her foot down about it."

In other words, Mom will kick his ass if he defies her. Neither of my parents is truly the head of the household. They share the responsibility unless it's a topic super important to one of them.

Then all bets are off.

"Son, I'm so sorry for getting the bastard the job. I should've been more thorough looking into him." My dad shakes his head, pain erupting in his exhausted features. "This is my fault. I let my guilt overrun common sense."

"There's no need to apologize. It's not your fault."

My dad's eyes are wet, and it eats at me to see him like this. "I should've protected my family better. But he's been taken care of."

His words are stern, his expression hard. He doesn't elaborate further, and I don't push because Killian will fill me in.

And I'm sure I can guilt my boyfriend into telling me even if my dad told him not to. I'll simply play the *I almost got killed* card. Killian will cave faster than a house of cards in a fucking hurricane.

Mom stirs awake, then makes her way to my bed, her heels clicking on the linoleum floor. She leans down and presses a gentle kiss to my forehead, her perfume enveloping me in its familiar scent. "You need anything, sweetheart?"

"To go home." I give her my best pleading look, but she just pins me with the mom look, the one that says *not a chance in hell, buddy*, then she turns to Killian. "Don't let me find out you snuck him out of here either, or you'll take a nice long swim next."

I blink a few times, then narrow my eyes, a smirk tugging at my lips. "Did a certain someone get a pair of cement shoes?"

Just then, a nurse comes in to check my vitals and the conversation dies off. She adjusts my IV bag and runs through some questions about how I'm feeling, her voice annoyingly chipper. I answer as best I can, gritting my teeth against the pain, and she finally leaves, closing the door behind her with a soft click.

"Well, this is nice and all . . ." I joke weakly, looking at my parents. "But you two need to meet Kill under better circumstances. Like, maybe dinner where no one's hooked up to machines and shit."

My dad looks from me to him. "Agreed, though we did spend some quality time together."

"Do I need to be jealous that you might be hitting on my boyfriend? He's mine and I'm not sharing."

Mom huffs and picks up her purse, slinging it over her shoulder. "Before this conversation goes somewhere utterly stupid, your father and I are going to go get some decent coffee. We'll be back in a little bit."

"Fuck you for rubbing decent food in my face." I pout, my stomach growling at the mention of anything edible.

Killian squeezes my hand. "Did you just . . . My mom would clock me if I cursed at her."

Mom just huffs. "Trust me, Killian, he knows better. By the way, would you like something? I can bring it back so you can eat it in front of my son, really rub it in."

Evil, vile woman.

"No thank you, Mrs. Reed." Kill smiles politely, ever the gentleman.

With that, my parents head out of the room, the door swinging shut behind them.

I try to sit up, wanting to get closer to Killian, but immediately the room spins, black spots dancing in my vision. I fall back against the pillows with a groan, my head pounding like a fucking jackhammer.

"Don't move too much." Killian's brows furrow as he smooths the hair back from my forehead. "You need to rest."

"You look like shit." I give him my best charming smile, ignoring the way it makes my split lip throb. "Now tell me how handsome I am. Boost my ego a little."

"Sorry, the hospital doesn't serve alcohol, so I'm pretty sober right now, and you're kinda busted-looking. Might take a pint or two before your mug starts to border on decent-looking."

"Worst boyfriend ever. You're lucky I love you."

"Took you long enough to say it back." Killian leans over and presses his mouth to mine in the gentlest of kisses. It's the only time we've ever been this soft with each other, and it makes my heart ache in the best way. He rests his forehead against mine, his breath ghosting over my skin. "I was terrified seeing you like this . . . When Alexei and Viktor came to SSU to get me . . ."

His voice trails off, and he swallows hard, his Adam's apple bobbing.

I squeeze his hand, the one he's still holding mine with, never having let go. "I'm okay. Or . . . at least I will be. I'm a stubborn bastard, remember?"

"I'm yours, Jackson. Every inch of me. Whatever you need, however you need it. I'm not going anywhere."

Killian's voice is fierce, his eyes blazing with determination and love.

His words send a flutter through my battered body, warmth coursing inside my veins like honey.

No matter how much pain I'm in, having Killian by my side makes me feel whole, like my world is complete.

Killian

EPILOGUE

I wince as the paintball hits my left ass cheek, the sting radiating through my body. And here I thought today would be a nice day after everything that went down two weeks ago. I mean, the Titans won the Frozen Four and it's surprisingly warm for April. Plus, Jackson's family lives in a goddamn mega-mansion right on the water.

But leave it to this asshole to ruin it.

"Are you kidding me right now?" I rub the sore spot, glaring daggers at my soon-to-be ex-boyfriend if he keeps this shit up, who's lounging on his king-sized bed like a smug ruler surveying his kingdom. The 1000 thread count sateen sheets beneath him shimmer in the soft light filtering through the floor-to-ceiling windows that overlook the bay.

My whole life I just thought sheets were sheets. But nope. Since Jackson got out of the hospital last week he's been staying at his family's house, and I got a lesson—aka a lecture—about proper thread count.

"I'm fucking stuck in this damn bed, and you've banned sex for the time being, so how else am I supposed to let the world know you're mine?" His lips curl into a wicked grin as he takes aim and shoots me again. This time the paintball hits me in the chest.

I stumble back, my hand flying to the spot where the ball made contact, the welt already forming beneath my fingertips. "Jackson, stop! You could've taken my eye out."

He scoffs, rolling his eyes. "Oh, please. I have perfect aim. And your nipple is nowhere near your eyeballs, dumbass."

"Swear to God I am going to break up with you . . . or push you off the damn bedroom balcony, you entitled fucktard."

"Maybe you should stop denying me sex then." He levels the gun at me, one eyebrow raised. "Are you going to ride my dick?"

A growl rips from my throat as I stalk toward him, ignoring the pain of another paintball hitting my shoulder. I rip the gun from his hands and march to the double French doors that lead out to the balcony, throwing them open with a bang. I step out into the unseasonably warm spring air, the salty breeze whipping through my hair as I yeet the gun over the railing, watching with satisfaction as it falls to the ground below.

After, I storm back into the room, then stand at the edge of the bed with my arms crossed. "Mind telling me why the fuck none of those balls broke?"

Jackson's eyes sparkle with mischief. "Viktor did me a solid and froze them. Turn around and pull down your pants. Let me see if there's a bruise forming on your ass."

I narrow my eyes, my voice low and threatening. "Keep acting up and see what happens."

He just waggles his eyebrows, unfazed by my anger. With a defeated sigh, I climb onto his oversized king bed, the mattress dipping beneath my weight as I crawl to sit next to him. "If you keep pushing me to go against the doctor's orders, I'm leaving your ass behind this summer."

Jackson's face tenses, his jaw clenching as he presses his lips into a thin, tight line, the Cupid's bow even more pronounced with the tense set of his facial muscles. "Not the first time you've made that threat, so if you don't want me going to Massachusetts with you, just say so."

"It's not that I don't want you to go." I swallow hard, the lump in my throat growing with each passing second. "What if . . . my mom . . . There's just no guarantee she'll have good days while you're there."

He grips my chin, tilting my head up until my eyes meet his. "Then *we* take care of her."

Now it's my turn to scoff. "Yeah, because that's what every guy wants to do on their vacation."

Jackson growls, his fingers tightening on my chin. "Kill, your family is mine. Your problems and fears are also mine. So, if that's how we spend two weeks, then so be it. You don't ever have to ask for help. You'll always have it without question."

Tears pool, spilling over and rolling down my cheeks no matter how hard I try to hold them back.

"Come on, jackass. You're going to make me stop saying nice things if this crying shit keeps happening." He teases, but his voice is soft, his touch gentle as he wipes away my tears with his thumb.

"Love you too, jackass," I whisper, a small smile tugging at the corners of my mouth.

I lean in and kiss him, claiming his mouth as he claims mine. His arms wrap around me, pulling me closer as the world outside fades away until it's just the two of us.

Jackson Reed will always be my biggest rival on the ice but off it, he's not just my boyfriend, he's my teammate in life.

And there's no one else I'd rather have by my side.

About the Author
E.V. OLSEN

E. V. Olsen is a romance author who loves to write about Over The Top alpha males who are possessive and completely obsessed with their person or mate. Nothing will get in their way from claiming what's theirs. She enjoys writing darker or angsty type romances whether in the contemporary world, PNR worlds, or even post-apocalyptic worlds.

Connect with E.V. Olsen online

EVOLSENBOOKS.WEEBLY.COM

TIKTOK.COM/@EVOLSENBOOKS

INSTAGRAM.COM/EVOLSENBOOKS

FACEBOOK.COM/EVOLSENBOOKS

Also By
E.V. OLSEN

Wasteland Temptations Series

Mine to Claim (Book 1)
Mine to Protect (Book 2)
His to Break (Book 3)
His to Lead (Book 4)

North Shore Titans Hockey Series

Savage Titan
Brutal Titan
Unhinged Titan
Ruthless Titan
Forbidden Titan

Made in United States
Troutdale, OR
01/18/2025

28074637R00090